Musical
MAYHEM

ALLEY CIZ

Also by Alley Ciz

BTU Alumni Series
Power Play (Jake and Jordan)
Musical Mayhem (Sammy and Jamie) BTU Novella
Tap Out (Gage and Rocky)
Sweet Victory (Vince and Holly)
Puck Performance (Jase and Melody)
Writing Dirty (Maddey and Dex)
Scoring Beauty (Ryan and Amara)
Defensive Hearts *Release TBD*

#UofJ Series
Cut Above The Rest (Prequel: Bette and E) <—Freebie.
Looking To Score (Kay and Mason)
Game Changer (Kay and Mason)
Playing For Keeps (Kay and Mason)
Off The Bench (Quinn and CK)
#UofJ5 *Release TBD*

The Royalty Crew (A #UofJ Spin-Off)
Savage Queen (Savvy and Jasper)
Ruthless Noble (Savvy and Jasper)

For all the friends who love no matter what and always have each others backs.

Text Handles

Sammy: THE SPIN DOCTOR
Jamie: ROCKSTAR MAN

The Coven
Maddey: QUEEN OF SMUT
Jordan: MOTHER OF DRAGONS
Skye: MAKES BOYS CRY
Rocky: ALPHABET SOUP
Becky: YOU KNOW YOU WANNA
Gemma: PROTEIN PRINCESS

Author Note

Dear Reader,
Musical Mayhem can be read as a stand-alone but it is
interconnected novella in the BTU Alumni world. For those of you
who have read my BTU books, you may have noticed Sammy from
Power Play *is married in* Tap Out. This is the story of how that
came about. You don't have to read Power Play *first but it might*
help you keep track of some of the crazy cast of characters as
large as The Coven and their guys.

So pump up those tunes and get ready to fall in love with my
boys.
XOXO
Alley

Chapter 1
Jamie

"I told you, man, I feel like maybe we need to take a break." I push the button on the elevator for our record label's floor.

"What do you mean we need a break?" Of course Andy sounds offended.

"Like break up the band?" Panic practically beats out of Steve's pores.

"You *can't* do that," Ian declares, always thinking he's in charge of the band.

Pete, our drummer and my closest friend, is the only one to stay silent as the lift jumps, speeding up the twenty-seven stories. In the reflection in the stainless steel doors, he looks almost bored.

Figures.

Our band, Birds of Prey, has been together since forever and were discovered back in high school—thank you, YouTube. We now have four multi-platinum albums, five Grammys, and more Billboard awards to our name than I can count. Our eclectic sound has made us a fan favorite spanning multiple genres.

But as the lead singer and front man, the pressure of putting out a good album always hits me harder than the others. It's just the way I'm wired.

"Of course I don't mean breaking up the band." With no wood in sight, I knock against the metal of the elevator car. "*God*, bro. Don't *even* put that out in the universe." I shudder at the thought.

Ding!

The doors open and we shuffle out. We're five minutes late, but if we don't make a pit stop in the kitchen for coffee—or in my case chamomile tea—this meeting will fail before it even begins.

"What I mean is…maybe we need to step back from this

album for a week or two. It might be what we need to get it to flow better, instead of the garbage it currently is."

We write all of our songs, and though it might drive some producers *insane*, we work closely with them to make sure our music is always true to our sound. In the beginning our label tried to push back, but record sales don't lie and money talks.

We may all be a *little* obsessed with the band Queen and Freddie Mercury's musical genius, but they held firm, and if you try to tell me "Bohemian Rhapsody" isn't one of the greatest songs of all time, you, my friend, are full of shit.

So what's the problem? We're old pros at this, right?

Wrong.

Our fifth album is pure crap. It is nowhere near where we want it to be, and with each producer brought in, we get further and further away from the right sound.

Music is as much, if not more, about the feeling it invokes as the notes it is comprised of.

Which brings us to today.

We are on producer number eight, with the label promising they found "the one."

Doubtful.

As a band we need a break, to get away to a beach or a mountain to snowboard. Anything really to wipe the slate clean and come back with fresh minds.

"Come on, Jame." Pete nudges me with an elbow, digging between my ribs. "Let's give the guy a chance."

I nod so he knows I heard him while telling myself if I'm not sold on this new candidate, I'll be on my private jet and flying off for a little R and R before the day is over.

Henry, one of the head A&R reps of the label, waits for us outside the conference room. Through the glass walls of the room I can see that, yup, we are definitely late.

Inside the room is a man with copper hair, and based on the dark gray MacBook Pro open on the table, I can only assume he is the producer that's been brought in.

He's tall, about an inch or two taller than my own six feet, and built like a linebacker.

He's on the phone, gesticulating and pacing. I can't tell if he's angry or not because I keep getting distracted by the pop and flex of muscles underneath the tight waffle weave of the black henley he is wearing.

Every hair on my body stands to attention.

Ummm... My mind stutters from the sight.

I can't tear my eyes away from him. The clothes do nothing to take away from the strength his muscles radiate. He's a big enough guy you would think he would come off clunky, as if you'd expect him to be some sort of bull in a china shop type, but his movements are graceful.

My gaze continues to sweep over his body, and I've never been more grateful for the low-backed chairs chosen for the conference room. Another pass of the room, and with this one I get the chance to appreciate one hell of a spectacular ass.

My hands itch with the need to grab it. My breath picks up like I ran the twenty-seven flights of stairs to get here, and my heart pounds like Pete's kick drum.

Ba-dum, ba-dum, ba-dum, ba-dum.

When he turns around again, he's smiling, the action lighting up his entire face as he continues his conversation. No way a person could be angry smiling like that.

You're still staring, Hawke.

Am I?

Shit! I am.

Look away. Look away now.

I have to physically force myself to look away. Not once can I recall ever having such an immediate and visceral reaction to a person before.

"—he's really great." The end of Henry's sentence finally registers as the rest of the spell I was under breaks.

Panic bubbles in my gut as I look over at my bandmates to see if they noticed. They didn't. I'm safe.

Phew.

You see...

I have a secret. A secret not even Pete knows. A secret harder to come by than a 1959 Gibson Les Paul Standard (Original Series) guitar.

I, Jamie Hawke, front man for BoP, rock star extraordinaire, am gay. I'm deep, *deep* inside my closet, but definitely gay. And this producer I'm potentially about to work with? He's *exactly* my type.

"I'm not making any promises," I say.

Henry holds up his hands as if to say *I'm not the enemy*. "I know, I know. There's no pressure. Just hear what Sammy has come up with and see if you want to proceed from there."

Sammy, huh? Looks like we already have something in common, both of us having unisex names.

Shit! Why the hell am I even thinking along those lines?

"What do you mean by listen to what he's come up with?" Ian sounds suspicious.

"You sent him our music?" Steve, as always, take the words right out of his mouth. The two of them are the most protective of our work. The idea of our uncut tracks sent to someone without our approval is a major no-go in their eyes.

"No, no, no." Henry's head whips back and forth in a panic. "He's done some producing work in the industry, but he's also a well-known DJ in the area. He has some originals to hear, as well as a portfolio of songs he's produced. Just relax and give the guy a chance."

I roll my shoulders back, needing to rid myself of the tension knotting them that has nothing to do with our music and everything to do with my secret. Waiting for the rest of my bandmates to enter, I take the last remaining seat on our side of the long black table.

Wheeling out one of the leather chairs, I try to focus on it and not Sammy. Of course, I fail spectacularly, and when a pair of warm caramel eyes turns my way, the breath stalls inside my lungs and time slows down.

What the hell?

"I gotta go, Madz. I'll see you later," he says into the

phone. "Yeah, I know. Love you too."

Like a boulder, my heart sinks. Of course he has a girlfriend. And why the hell do I feel such an overwhelming crush of disappointment at the realization?

So what if I'm attracted to him? Heart-pounding, breath-catching, ball-tingling attraction doesn't mean it's reciprocated. He doesn't give off any "gay vibes"—eye roll, please, at how fucking dumb that phrase is, but who the hell am I to judge? I've practically set up residency in the walk-in closet I hide in.

Besides, it doesn't matter if he's gay anyway. Not like I can do anything about it.

Like every other day for the last twenty-six years, I swallow down my feelings, burying any thoughts or attraction deep behind the mental clothes a person saves for *when they'll fit again* and firm up the front I put on for the world.

Chapter 2

Sammy

I'm so nervous I feel like I'm going to throw up. I have no idea who or how my name got mentioned to the Birds of Prey's people, but holy shit, I'm still pinching myself at the possibility of working with one of the biggest rock bands since the Rolling Stones, Queen, or Led Zeppelin.

Thank god Maddey is the *best* best friend a person could ask for. When the band was late, I called her to distract me.

She talks.

I pace and try and forget how important this interview could be for my career.

"So, yeah. Like I was saying, you are perfect for the cover I have in mind. I need you. Well, you and Skye. And you're my best friend, so you can't tell me no."

I have to bite into the fleshy part of my palm to hold back the laughter her usual mile-a-minute way of speaking brings on. Homegirl is barely over five feet. Even physics says it's impossible for that much energy to fit into such a small package. But no one, I mean *no one*, tells Maddey McClain she can't do something.

If that *something* has to do with one of the best-selling romance novels she writes? Well, *all* bets are off. Our group of friends has learned not to question, comment, or ask when she gets an idea. It's safer that way. Safer = not being added as a character to one of her books and being killed off.

"Madz," I cut in, "you know I'll do whatever you need. For most my life I haven't been able to say no to you. What makes you think I can start now?"

"Have I told you I loved you today?"

"Yup, but you know you can tell me as often as you'd like, and I won't complain."

Movement by the door catches my attention, and the five members of Birds of Prey filter into the room, taking seats around the conference table. Time to cut this conversation off, because if I don't, lord knows she could go on until her phone battery dies.

"I gotta go, Madz. I'll see you tonight."

"Okay, I'll meet you at the Garden."

My breath releases at her quick acceptance to meet up for the hockey game tonight. When a good chunk of your friends play professional hockey, you spend a considerable amount of your free time in hockey arenas.

"Love you most." This has been how she's said goodbye to me all our lives. It was a way to make me feel special amongst her three older brothers.

"Yeah, I know. Love you too."

My concern over being taken as rude is unfounded because none of them are paying me any attention. They are talking amongst themselves—all except one.

My lungs seize as the striking set of violet eyes belonging to the band's sex-on-legs front man locks on me.

I've never really had a type, more a live and let live, let the tide take me on my journey of *love*, but Jamie Hawke—*oh boy*, he's something else.

If you looked up sexy rock star in the dictionary, his picture would be there, with his inky black hair styled in a faux hawk, close-cropped beard groomed with sharp slashes underneath model-worthy cheekbones, and full sleeves of colorful tattoos.

Tattoos that extend around to his defined pecs and across his broad shoulders.

The record in my brain screeches as I cut those thoughts

off. The *last* thing I need is to get caught lusting over a client—my *straight* client.

I need to hit up a bar with Maddey later.

Henry, my label contact, speaks. "Gentlemen, this is Sammy Rhodes. He's worked with a few key players in the industry but originally made a name for himself locally in the club circuit as The Spin Doctor."

He goes on to list some of the bigger names I've had the privilege to work with over the years. With each mention, the appreciation on the bandmates' faces grows. I'm damn proud of how I've been able to parlay my DJing career into music production, but working with BoP would be *the* feather in my metaphorical cap.

"Henry told us you have samples for us to listen to?" the rhythm guitarist, Ian, asks.

"You have anything you haven't released yet?" Steve the bass player's blue eyes light up at the possibility of hearing something exclusive.

Mulling over my current catalog, I end with a shake of my head. "I don't have any specific tracks in the works. My latest project is more of a passion project for one of my friends."

"Can we hear it?" This question comes from lead guitarist, Andy.

"Sure." I shrug, pulling up the program I use to create mixes. I scroll through my files to the most recent and click it open, the first notes of the *Superman* theme song sounding through the laptop's speakers.

The original theme from the '70s is the base, and I beefed up the horns and trumpets. The music shifts, the pounding beat of bass pulsing underneath, the intensity building into the perfect crescendo for when Vince would make his entrance.

"Superhero buff?" Pete looks from me, then to the only person who hasn't uttered a word yet—Jamie.

"I guess…but my buddy I made this for sure is." A click of a button cuts it off. "I've been toying around with the track for a few days. He needs something more befitting of his entrance."

"Entrance?"

Shit.

Now I'm second-guessing choosing this specific track as an example. I may keep company with a number of pretty famous athletes, but I don't want to come across as a name-dropper to a group of rock and roll royalty. It's probably the *last* thing they want in a producer.

Real smooth, Rhodes.

I blame the faux pas on those violet eyes. They're enough to make any person lose their train of thought. I'm only human.

"Yeah." I run a hand through my hair, tugging on the strands to center myself. "I thought he needed something more when he eventually makes a run for the UFC's Light Heavyweight belt."

I try—and fail—to look away from Jamie. The sudden flare of excitement lighting his eyes makes it impossible.

"You're talking about Vince Steele, aren't you?" Interest bleeds from his words.

"You'll have to forgive my friend," Pete jumps in with a laugh. "He's a *huge* MMA junkie. He knows *all* the entrance music for the top contenders."

"Fuck off, man."

What the hell is with this sudden urge to come to Jamie's defense? It's almost an ache to make things better.

"No judgment here. I am too. I mean…I guess I don't have much of choice seeing as I've been friends with the guy since college, but that's why I'm working on it for him."

"Can you play it again?" Jamie asks.

I don't know if it's the mixed martial arts connection, or if Jamie honestly liked what he heard, but I'm not going to look a gift horse in the mouth. If rock god Jamie Hawke wants to listen to my tracks, I'm going to play them.

Chapter 3

Jamie

The headphones swing to and fro from the mic stand as I make my way out of the sound booth into the connected room, still unsure if hiring Sammy Rhodes was the best or *worst* decision I've ever made.

From a musical perspective, it is undeniably the best. The album has come along more in one day than we've been able to accomplish in three months. The way he's plucked beats and tweaked parts is so seamless, it's almost like he's the sixth member of the band.

My earlier concerns over the album are laughable. If the rest of our sessions go even remotely like this one, the album will be complete on time, if not early.

My only remaining professional concern stems from how Sammy has the potential to blow up my career on a personal level. As a closeted gay man, tamping down my attraction is normal, but the temptation Sammy poses teeters me closer to tipping over.

The entire time I was in the booth, I couldn't take my eyes off him and his broad shoulders. I noticed everything about him. The way his copper-colored hair constantly flopped over his brow when he concentrated on the sound dials of the mixing board, or how he absentmindedly brushed it out of the way when it did.

"Should I play it back?" Sammy asks as we spread out amongst the couches and chairs on his side, the deep timbre of his voice washing over me like a melody.

He's straight.

My lips turn down at the reminder of this crucial detail.

With the push of a button, the upbeat tempo of Steve's bass fills the room until it's joined by Ian's guitar. The two instruments weave together, and by the time the quick pattern of Pete on the drums joins in with the riff of Andy's guitar, anyone listening would want to dance.

Even without the words, I know Sammy feels the track. His head bobs unconsciously along, the same way it did while we recorded. It's adorable.

Adorable? What the fuck?

A glance at the clock reveals it's late enough to call it a day without raising suspicions. I need to put some distance between me and this specimen of male perfection before I do something I can't take back.

"So much for taking a break, huh, Jame?" Pete gives me a knowing smirk.

Startled caramel eyes find me, and everything else fades away.

Sonofabitch.

"Fuck no!" Ian breaks the spell. "Looks like we found our mojo." He points to a still-wide-eyed Sammy.

"You guys were thinking of breaking up?" Sammy's words are tinged with panic.

"No!" I rush out. A driving need to ease away the worry pulses inside, unlike the blah I felt when the others expressed a similar concern. "These idiots just like to jump to conclusions."

"Divas," Pete states.

"Divas is for chicks. What's the male version?" Andy asks.

"Well, according to Queen B, it's a hustler." Sammy flashes his should-be-illegal-it-is-so-gorgeous smile.

"Oh, I like you," Steve declares with his famous shit-eating grin. "First, you save our album from jumping off the ledge, and now you're speaking in music references. Yup, I say we keep you."

I want to keep you.

Well, shit.

Thoughts like these are going to get me in trouble. It's been way too long since I've had a release that didn't come from my own hand. That has to be the reason behind these asinine *feelings*.

Hooking up with women may not be my preferred method of getting off, but desperate times call for desperate measures. If I don't, I'm liable to do something stupid.

"Well." I push to stand. "I don't know about you boys, but I could use a drink."

A round of agreements meet my announcement. The Birds of Prey never turn down a cold one in a hole-in-the-wall dive bar. Just what I was counting on.

"Wanna join, Rhodes?" Pete extends the invitation, always playing the role of our social director.

"Maybe next time." Sammy rises from his wheeled chair. "I'm already at risk of being late to The Garden as it is."

"Storm fan?"

"Blizzards." Those broad shoulders rise in a shrug, once again drawing my eye.

"Aww, man. Pete, you're falling down on the job not getting us rivalry tickets." Ian playfully shoves him, setting off the others.

Thanks to my dumbass bandmates acting like the human equivalent of bumper cars, I'm knocked into Sammy and would have gone tumbling ass over teakettle if he hadn't steadied me with both hands wrapping around my biceps.

Electricity chases down my spine at his touch. He affects me like no one else.

His gaze scans me up and down, making sure I'm good. He's so close I notice he has a thin ring of yellow around his pupils. The way it swirls together with the orange surrounding it makes me think of melted caramel on ice cream.

I need to get out of the room—immediately.

Chapter 4

Sammy

Fiddling with the controls of the sound board, I search for the perfect balance of bass and treble so Pete's drums don't overpower the husky timbre of Jamie's voice in the ballad.

Two weeks into working with the band and we already have four completed tracks, and if I can get the levels on this one sorted, we'll have five.

Another adjustment…and…there, perfect.

Aside from being a huge fan, working with them has been more of a dream come true than I could have ever expected. One would think a band as successful as theirs would be full of egos a person would have to navigate around like a carefully crafted dance, but there is none of that.

Surprisingly, hanging with them reminds me a lot of my own squad. If anyone gets too big for their britches, there is always someone there to knock them back down to reality.

Now if only someone could knock some sense into me. Because with each day that passes, the attraction I feel toward Jamie increases.

What the hell is with that?

I'm surrounded by ripped bodies of professional athletes on a weekly basis—perks of being besties with the women who run the professional lives of hockey players and MMA fighters— but not once have I ever had a *draw* like this to a straight male. I can't make heads or tails of it.

"Oh." The startled sound of the man in question rings out as he enters the room. "I didn't think anyone was still here."

My grin is automatic. How is it that a man who has performed in front of tens of thousands in sold-out arenas and stadiums around the world is so socially awkward? And why does it have to be so damn charming?

"Yeah, sorry." I straighten in my chair, taking in how good Jamie looks in his tight black CBGBs t-shirt, the bright colors of his tattoos enhanced by the dark cotton. "I wanted to put the final touches on the track before heading out."

"There's no rush." He grins, and it hits me in all the feels.

"I know." I run a hand through my hair for something to do, moving my eyes off the tempting singer to the mixing board. "There was just this spot in the song I wanted to tweak while the idea was fresh in my mind."

"You know." He walks over and settles into the chair next to me, my pulse spiking from his nearness. "The guys always accuse *me* of being the perfectionist when we record, but you might have me beat."

The light, fresh scent of his cologne invades my senses, inviting me to breathe deeper. *God, he smells good.*

"Can I hear?" He points to the board.

"Sure." Our hands brush, sparks shooting up my arm from the touch before hitting the button to queue up the section I'd been tweaking.

At Jamie's hiss, I quickly pull away before making him uncomfortable.

We're silent as the ballad swells and retreats like waves on a beach. We make eye contact as the song reaches its climax, and his eyes sparkle like amethysts with excitement.

"Fuck." He runs a hand over his scruff, the scratchy sound of sandpaper filling the room.

What would it feel like under my hands?

"It's like you're *inside* my head."

"Thanks," I say sheepishly. "I think it helps that I'm a

genuine fan of the band."

"Whatever it is, it's magic." Another pass over his scruff. "It's no wonder you were so successful as a DJ. I think some of your remixes are better than the originals."

Say what now?

"You've heard my stuff?" I would have thought the only thing he would have cared about were the songs I produced, not my originals.

"Yup. I found your SoundCloud account. You're good— *really* good."

"Thanks." My cheeks heat at the unexpected compliment coming from someone so accomplished in the music industry.

"Why switch to producing? From what I've read you could have been the next David Guetta or Calvin Harris. Why the change to a more behind-the-scenes role?"

He researched me? Does that mean he's interested in me?

Don't be a dumbass. He hired you for a job—of course he's going to look up your qualifications. What the hell is wrong with you, Rhodes?

It's never a good thing when I start berating myself in the third person. I've officially lost my mind. I need a Coven intervention stat. Though the six of them might not be much help. I love my ladies dearly, but they are the definition of trouble.

Lord knows Maddey would be all for pushing me to pursue something with Jamie, all in the name of book research of course. My bestie hasn't met a forbidden romance trope she hasn't liked.

"To be honest, I kind of just fell into the whole DJing thing on accident. I guess it almost goes hand in hand with producing, but I never expected to be known for it the way I am. To me it was more of a way to make some money while in college."

"Makes sense." He crosses an ankle over his knee, and why the hell is that move so sexy?

Fuck. Mind out of the gutter, asshole.

This is the first time in the weeks I've been here he seems to be settling in to have a conversation instead of rushing off. At times he gives off the impression of being uncomfortable around me, but for the life of me I can't figure out why that would be.

I'm not sure what changed, but I'll take it.

"It was easy too. I was already going out; it just sort of evolved into going out wherever I was spinning instead. It was a win-win for us all."

"What changed?"

What did change?

"I guess I'm getting old and I didn't want to spend all of my weekends in the club anymore."

He snorts.

"*Old?*" He quirks a brow, the move way too cute on him. "Aren't you a few years younger than me? I guess I should trade in my mic stand for a walker if you're old."

"You mean you don't want to be strutting across the stage, rocking out like Keith?" No one rocked harder than the legendary front man of the Rolling Stones.

"I wish I had his energy." Another snort escapes and this playful side coming out is intriguing as hell. "By the time we get halfway through a tour, I'm ready to run away and sleep for a week. I have *no* idea how he still does it."

"I bet... I tag along with some of my friends for Blizzards road games, but that's only for a day or two. I couldn't imagine what it's like moving from city to city for months on end."

"Wow. That big of a fan?"

How to answer?

Hockey may not have anything to do with music, but the players I'm connected to are some of the most famous in the league.

"My old college roommate is married to one of the players. I tag along with her sometimes when she travels for games."

"Your roommate was a girl?"

"Three of them actually." My smile is automatic like anytime I remember the one year we all lived together. "We rented an apartment my sophomore year. It was... *interesting.*"

"It's gotta be better than living with a group of guys though. I swear the tour bus is like a frat house on wheels."

As if they know I'm talking about them, my phone starts to vibrate so much it falls from the mixing board. Based on the number of notifications coming through across the screen, it can only mean the ladies added me to one of their "Coven Conversations."

I'll wait to read their texts. The way the six of them switch topics and go off on tangents is NSFW, and the last thing I need is to have a witness to their epic inappropriateness.

I wouldn't trade them for the world.

Besides, the interruption is a blessing. Seeing this new side to Jamie only makes me notice things I shouldn't. Like how his smile is a little bit crooked when he really lets loose, or how his laughter is as melodic as his singing.

"Damn." It's gotten later than I thought. "I gotta go."

"Sure. Okay. Yeah, I'll walk out with you."

That wasn't disappointment was it? Right?

Chapter 5

Jamie

One month.

One *long* month of dealing with feelings and urges unlike anything I had ever experienced in my life. From a production standpoint, we've never been this productive or ahead of schedule ever, but I start to wonder if it's going to come at the cost of my sanity.

I've taken more women to bed in the last thirty days than I have this *year*, all in an effort to forget about Sammy Rhodes.

If only it worked.

You wouldn't think sneakers made a sound on concrete, but each one of my steps booms in my ears as I pace in front of Sammy's building. The doorman hasn't stopped eyeing me warily from behind the glass entranceway.

I don't blame him. I'm sure I'm coming off as a crazy person.

I shouldn't be here.

This is a mistake.

Honestly? I couldn't tell you what possessed me to show up here.

Wait, that's a lie. Yes, yes I do know.

Sammy Rhodes is temptation incarnate. *Never* have I felt a pull, a *draw*, like I do to my new producer.

It doesn't help that the band loves the guy. The few times he's joined us for a drink at the bar, I've had to cut out early. I'm like a moth to a fucking flame with him. Except touching it would burn so much more than me. The band shouldn't have to pay because I'm struggling to keep my dick in my pants.

The work connection is one hurdle; the fact the guy is straight makes the issue a nonstarter. Yet here I stand, like an asshole, trying to work up the nerve to ring up temptation's apartment.

Was this really the best idea I could come up with? Do I really think if maybe I spend time one-on-one with Sammy I won't like him and that it's just lust pulling me toward him? Hell if I know. At this point I'm willing to try anything.

I really should have my head checked because *clearly* I'm losing it.

Taking a breath, I stare at the high-rise. My new obsession is obviously good at what he does if he's able to afford such a luxurious building.

Okay, Hawke. Time to grow a set.

Tucking my hands in the pockets of my leather jacket, I walk the final ten feet to the entrance, shooting the doorman a sheepish smile as I pass. Guy's been watching me for twenty minutes—gotta give him credit for not calling the cops.

The lobby is as nice as I expected while I did my best to wear a path in the cement. The floor is Italian marble, the reception desk glass and chrome.

Even under the brim of my Yankees hat, I don't miss the spark of recognition from the man behind the counter. Hopefully I can use it to my advantage.

"Evening, Mr. Hawke."

Give the man points for keeping it professional.

"Evening." I worry the brim in my hands, tugging it so it shifts back and forth on my skull.

"How can I help you?"

Toeing the marble with my sneaker, indecision once again courses through me.

Should I stay or should I go?

And damn it, now I have The Clash stuck in my head.

"I'm here to see Sammy Rhodes?"

Why did I say that like a question?

Confusion crosses his face, and I have a mini panic attack that he knows *why* I've sought out Sammy, before mentally rolling my eyes at my own lunacy. My paranoia is growing the longer I keep my true self hidden.

But look how nice my closet is. It's one of those kinds that's big enough to have a seating area and everything.

I'm about to say *screw it* and leave when his face brightens in recollection. "Oh yes." He nods. "Mr. Rhodes is staying in one of our penthouses. If you'll forgive me, I'll have to call up to announce you since you aren't on the list."

"I understand." I wave off the concern, familiar with the protocol.

Pulling out my phone, I thumb through the band's social media while waiting to hear if I'm allowed entry or if this whole thing was a fool's errand.

Entry or not, you are a fool. You're playing with fire, man.

"Oh," I hear him say with surprise. "Evening, Miss McClain. It's Tobias from downstairs."

Great, the girlfriend is here. I really didn't think this through at all. I'm an idiot. I should go.

"I have a guest here to see Mr. Rhodes." He grins as he listens to whatever is being said on the other line before his gaze lifts to me. "I have a Mr. Jamie Hawke."

Tobias chuckles as he continues to listen.

"Very well. I will send him right up. Have a nice night, Miss McClain."

Following the directions to the correct elevator, it's like my shoes have become cinder blocks and not old-school Jordans.

My skin feels two sizes too small as the internal war continues. It's too late to flee. They know I'm here; leaving would only raise questions I can't even begin to answer.

Questions like why you're here, maybe? Let me go pop some popcorn, this shit is better than reality TV. My inner voice sounds a lot like Pete at the moment.

I heave out a sigh. Maybe coming face-to-face with the girlfriend will finally help squash the crush I've been developing on the boyfriend.

Seriously, I couldn't be more stupid if I tried.

Hand raised, I hesitate for time one million and one. *Stupid, stupid, stupid.*

Filling my lungs like prepping to belt out a killer note, I do it—I knock.

There are three beeps and the door starts to open while I brace for the first glimpse of Sammy's girlfriend or the man himself.

Party-level noise filters out into the hall—I did not picture Sammy to be a partier—as the door continues to open and I'm left facing…Jase Donnelly?

As a resident of Manhattan whenever the band isn't touring, it's no surprise I recognize the blond Hemsworth-looking man in front of me. There's a billboard of his across from BoP's in the center of Times Square, and when I say Pete is the Storm's biggest fan, it isn't an exaggeration.

Pete is going to revoke my best-friend card when he finds out I met the Storm defenseman and didn't call him. In my defense, I couldn't tell him I was here without being questioned why I was there in the first place.

I should change my name to Charlotte with the complicated web of lies I weave.

What I don't get is *why* Jase Donnelly is answering the door to Sammy's apartment? And what the hell is with the shit-eating grin?

"Holy shit." His hazel eyes widen. "When Madz said it was you downstairs, I would have sworn Tobias was pulling our leg."

I'm speechless, rooted on the spot. He's not the only one unsure how to process what they see.

Forget the vowel—can I buy a clue please?

"Come in." He pulls the door wider. "I doubt you came here to see the hallway."

With a nod, I step into the small foyer.

"Sammy!" he shouts into the apartment. "Hurry your ass up, there's someone here to see you." He stretches out a hand. "Jase."

"Jamie."

Shouts and curses come from behind Jase, and he chuckles.

"Oh, I know. I'll try not to squeal like a fangirl, but I can't make any promises about Madz."

"I heard that, Trip." My body tenses as a feminine voice calls out from somewhere in the apartment.

"You were meant to," he yells back. "Want a beer or anything?" He nods for me to follow.

The penthouse is gorgeous and huge by New York standards. The living room, kitchen, and dining room are all visible thanks to the open-concept layout, and there's one hell of a view out the floor-to-ceiling windows.

"I'd say yes if I were you." Sammy rounds the corner into the kitchen and holy shit.

I have to check my chin for drool because—*damn*. The quick glimpse of six-pack abs and black ink I get before they're covered by a light gray BTU Hockey t-shirt can only be classified as drool-worthy.

"You might need the lubrication for the crazy you are about the step into." Those caramel eyes crinkle at the corners as he smiles, already holding out a beer in offering.

Accepting the green bottle on instinct, my mind trips over the word *lubrication*. Again all the reasons I shouldn't have come run through my mind—*clearly* it's forever in the gutter around Sammy.

"Someone's got jokes," another voice calls out, bringing our attention to the living room filled with people. Are they playing Mario Kart?

What am I getting myself into?

"So…" Sammy leans a hip against the counter. "Don't take this as you not being welcome here or anything…but what are you doing here?"

"Umm…" I look around the penthouse, trying to figure out *how* to answer the question. I don't think telling him I'm hoping if I spend enough time with him I won't want to bend him over the mixing board anymore.

"You know what?" Sammy waves off the question like the reasoning doesn't matter. "Come on." He nods toward the room. "I'll introduce you to part of my squad. Just don't hold them against me."

I'd like to hold you against me.

Fuck.

Fuck.

Fuck!

Stop fucking thinking like that, Hawke.

"Guys," Sammy calls for their attention. "This is Jamie. Please keep in mind I *technically* work for him, and don't embarrass me too much."

The second part comes out in a rush, and I think it's the first time I've witnessed him uncomfortable.

"So, you met Jase." He waves a hand at the hockey player, then to a trio of women scattered throughout the room. "These are some of my girls—Skye, Rocky, and Maddey."

I'm surprised he doesn't make a more formal introduction for his girlfriend but relieved I don't have to play nice yet.

You really are an asshole, Hawke.

That teasing grin is back on Sammy's face as takes a few steps to the right. "And I know you recognize this fool over here." He claps Vince Steele on the shoulder.

Well, shit. Now I'm the one at risk of fangirling. Fangirling? Wouldn't it be fanboying? Not the point.

I've followed the fighter's career from the beginning, so shaking his hand is all kinds of surreal.

"Can I tell you how full of shit I thought our boy here was"—Vince claps Sammy on the shoulder—"when he told me Jamie-Fucking-Hawke knew who *I* was?"

"Vin, stop being a fanboy." I recognize the girl tugging on his arm as his sister Rocky from his fights.

What? I told you I was a fan, and it is fanboying—good to know.

"Yeah, it's embarrassing," comes from Skye.

"*Seriously*. At least pretend like you've met a celebrity before. You're making us all look bad," another blonde says, walking into the room from down the hall.

"How's our older brother doing?" Jase filters into the room behind her with a fresh round of beers.

"How the hell would I know?" She accepts the lone bottle of water with a smile.

"You *were* just on the phone with him."

"Umm…no. I was having phone sex with my husband to get him amped for the game. These West Coast games kill me with time zones."

I have the misfortune of taking a sip of beer during that little announcement. I swear she just mentioned phone sex the same way one would say what they had for dinner.

Sammy pats my back, his hand hitting just beneath my shoulder blades, in an effort to help expel the liquid from the wrong pipe. I'm no longer focused on my near IPA drowning, because all my focus is on those tingles I feel when we touch.

"You alright?" Sammy asks as Jase cries out, "TMI."

I nod, clearing my throat as the last of the coughing subsides.

"Told ya you were about to step into a whole lot of crazy. I've tried to shake them but haven't had much success through the years. I think I'm stuck with them."

"Stop spreading lies about us," the newer blonde chastises. "Don't believe a word he says. I'm Jordan by the way." She holds out a hand to shake before joining the ongoing conversation inside the living room.

It takes a moment, but eventually the realization of who she is hits me. I move a few steps closer to Sammy and say, "So when you said you had a friend whose husband played for the Blizzards, you neglected to mention it was Jordan Donnelly-Donovan." Her husband, Jake, is one of the best goalies in the

NHL right now and will probably be selected to represent the USA in the Olympics this winter.

Most family members of athletes aren't recognizable on their own, but she is. The Donnelly family has one hell of a pedigree—they're like the Mannings of hockey. You'd be hard-pressed to find someone with more NHL connections than Jordan.

"She technically didn't hyphenate." Those caramel eyes are dancing in amusement.

"*That's* the part you want to focus on here? How is it you don't brag even a little bit?"

I'm flabbergasted. I *cannot* believe he has not said one word about this. Pete is going to lose his fucking mind.

"They're my friends." He shrugs, and again I'm distracted by the way the seams of his shirt strain.

"They're professional athletes."

"Says the rock star."

Touché.

"Yeah, yeah, yeah, we're awesome. The best thing since sliced bread and all that." Jase twists around to lean over the couch. "Can we please get to the *important* questions now?"

Shit! Is he gonna ask why I'm here? Sammy let it go before—will I be able to avoid the question a second time?

"What's that?" I ask as if I'm not seconds away from a panic attack.

"You any good at Mario Kart?" He holds out a miniature steering wheel controller.

"I've been known to hold my own." Aside from writing music, video games were the preferred method of passing time on the tour bus.

I accept the offering, my gaze landing on the one female who has yet to speak to me—Maddey. Damn, she is beautiful. She's a pixie of a girl, with a riot of long blonde curls and ice-blue eyes. It's easy to see why Sammy dates her. If I were *actually* into girls, I'd hit on her.

"Perfect." Jase beams like a fan backstage at a BoP concert.

"Come on." Another touch from Sammy zaps through me before he directs us to an area on the massive sectional. "Be warned. Madz is a ringer."

"Hey!" Her jaw drops in offense as she stands so Sammy can sit. "I don't recall you complaining when I used my superior driving skills to win us beer money every week in college."

"These are your old roommates?" My voice comes out strained watching Maddey settle herself on Sammy's lap so we can all fit.

The two of them are the picture-perfect couple. I want to hate her on principle alone but can't help but be charmed when she flashes me with a set of dimples.

Wait? I thought he said he lived with three girls?

"Yeah." He eases back on the couch, our thighs brushing with the movement. Something I shouldn't be enjoying when his girlfriend is perched on the other. "Well, not Rocky. She wasn't a part of our house of crazy."

"Nope. But I do live in one of my own, so…"

It's like an entire conversation happens as Rocky's words trail off.

"Is college where you all met?" I'm intrigued and need to know more.

"Yes and no," he answers, that section of hair flopping forward.

My hands fist in an effort not to reach out and brush it back, my molars grinding when Maddey is the one to do so.

"Madz and I grew up together. We met Skye and Jordan our freshman year at NYU."

"You didn't go there?" I point at his BTU Titans shirt.

"No."

"But we consider both him and Madz honorary BTU alums with how much time they spent at our school after JD and Skye transferred," Jase explains, jerking a chin at Jordan and Skye.

"The rest of our squad all went to BTU. It's only fair to include them," Rocky adds.

"Oh man, they are going to be jealous when they hear

about you showing up tonight." A satisfied smirk plays on Skye's lips as she selects Toad as her avatar.

"There's *more* of you?"

How is that possible?

"Yup. This isn't even half of our crew," Jase says.

The seven people inside the penthouse already outnumber the entire band.

"Just be grateful you aren't meeting *all* of The Coven tonight." Vince scrolls to pick Bowser.

"The Coven?" I choke out. Am I going to have to drink some Kool-Aid or something? I quickly scan their feet to make sure they aren't all wearing matching sneakers or anything.

"Ignore him." Rocky shakes her head. "It's just some stupid nickname the guys gave us."

"Besides," Maddey cuts in, and I try not to be jealous of her, "Sammy is an honorary member."

"Yeah," Jordan agrees. "Don't go making us look bad in front of the rock star. Now, time to put your money where your mouth is, Steele. Pick your character, and let's see if Jamie is better about losing to a bunch of girls than you are."

I get the feeling that Jordan is considered the group's default leader, and I wouldn't want to face her wrath. Pushing the Down arrow button until I land on Donkey Kong, I settle in to make Rainbow Road—oh the irony—my bitch.

I have a feeling I'm going to need to prove myself here. All to a group I never saw coming.

Chapter 6

Sammy

"Fuck yeah!" Vince stands to do the running man in celebration as Jamie's Donkey Kong nudges out Maddey's Princess Peach for the win. "*Finally*, someone able to beat the queen."

I swear I'm dreaming. There is no way this is real life. No one would believe that Jamie-*Fucking*-Hawke has spent the last hour playing video games with my friends.

"You act like I never lose, Vin." Maddey rises from my lap and passes off her controller to Jordan before heading into the kitchen for another round of beers.

"This is true. But he beat you *four* times." He holds up four fingers as if we can't count.

"I can't even with you."

"Nope. I gotta agree with my boy here. Sorry, Jamie, you can no longer tour," Jase jumps in, amping up Vince. "Your new job is to beat Tink at Mario Kart forever and ever."

"Are they always like this?" Jamie leans in to ask, bringing his intoxicating scent with him.

Using the boisterousness of the crazies in my life as an excuse, I lean in too, eliminating the remaining space between us. Just because nothing can develop from my crush doesn't mean I'm not going to enjoy the perks of being around him.

I think I'm more surprised he showed up to begin with than *why* he did. The times I've gone out with the band I've gotten the impression he wanted to be anywhere else. So to seek me out? I don't know, nor do I care.

"This is tame compared to when we're all together. Vince and Jase are bad, but when they get together with our friends Tucker and Becky, all bets are off—prank wars ensue."

I expected him to shift away. Instead his head tilts, those amethyst eyes bouncing over my face, making butterflies take flight in my stomach the longer he stares.

"And I thought going on tour was insane."

"If you keep coming around, you'll see. You might regret picking me to produce your album, but I can guarantee you won't be bored."

Those butterflies beat their wings as if they are the size of Dumbo's ears. I want him to come around—a lot. More than I should really. But it's not like things have the potential to develop past friendship, because *Jamie is straight.*

Seriously. The Coven needs to come up with an intake form because I need to be rehabilitated from this bad habit I'm forming.

"You do realize once the band finds out Jase Donnelly hangs out at your place, they are going to be inviting themselves over all the time?" That lopsided smirk makes an appearance.

I probably shouldn't tell him how much I like the way that sounds. It's math I can get behind. Jamie Hawke plus being around all the time? Sign me the fuck up.

It takes a moment for the rest of what he said to register.

"This isn't my apartment."

A v forms between his dark brows, and I want to smooth it away.

Don't you fucking touch him, Rhodes.

"But it was listed in your contact info."

It all clicks.

"So…*that's* how you found me. Stalker much," I tease.

"Well… Uhh…" A blush tints his cheeks, the reaction endearing, humanizing the untouchable rocker.

"I'm kidding, Jam. Relax."

"Jam?"

I shrug. "We're kinda big on nicknames and shorthands in this group if you haven't picked up on it."

"But why not Jame like the other guys?"

Another shrug. "No idea. But I think Jam works. Unless you don't?"

A different sort of smile spreads across his face. "No, it works…Spins."

My face is at risk of cracking my smile gets that big. I may have the most inconvenient crush on the guy, but *damn*, it wasn't going to take away from how special this moment is.

"Okay." Jamie keeps his head bent close. "Tell me how you ended up with Jase Donnelly's apartment listed as your place of residence?"

"I'll give you the CliffsNotes version or else we'll be here all night." Not that that scenario would be much of a hardship.

Glancing around the apartment, each one of my people are doing their own thing. Though technically we are all guests at Jase's, none of us act like it. No matter whose place we are in, we all treat it as our home.

"The truth is…we are a very incestuous group." Beer sprays me in the face as Jamie sputters. Yes, I went for shock value.

"Wh-what?"

He's adorable all confused like.

"I don't mean literally." I can't help but laugh. "Most of us are connected in more ways than one."

I start to explain the multiple connections.

Jordan: sibling to Jase, married to his old college teammate, my old roommate, manages all the PR for the athletes in our group with Skye, Covenette.

Jase: sibling to Jordan, dated Rocky, has a four-bedroom apartment, so anyone in our group has a place to stay when we are in the city.

Maddey's head pops in between us before I can go on to add how she is connected not just by being my childhood friend and the roommate situation, but that she dated Jordan's older brother, Ryan.

I'm in the middle of clearing her blonde curls from my face when she goes in for the kill—AKA enlisting her next victim in her writing inspiration.

Oh man. Jam has no idea what is about to come his way.

Maddey is one of the most charming people on the planet. He might not realize it, but he's about to say yes to things he could never imagine being asked, let alone agreeing to.

"So, question." I can't see her face, but I know she has her dimples out in full force. Her older brothers may be big badass military men, but even they crumble under them.

Jamie's panicked eyes bounce between me and my best friend, obviously looking for a life jacket. I'd help him, but twenty-four years of experience has taught me not to bother trying to get in between Maddey and one of her ideas.

"Ever since Samz started working with you guys, no matter how much I've told them to stay in their lane, I cannot shut the rock stars up."

Those violet irises are now tinged with *am I about to about to get stabbed by a crazy person?*

"Madz is a romance author," I explain.

"Yeah, and she exploits us all for her personal gain," Jase quips.

Skye snorts. "Like you don't bust out the books you're on the covers of and brag."

"Umm…" Jamie attempts to answer, but like most people when thrust into our crazy, words are hard to come by.

"It's okay, I speak fluent Maddey." I ruffle her hair, and she shifts to rest her head on my shoulder, not caring she's still hanging over the back of the couch. "She wants to know if it would be alright if she crashes one of BoP's recording sessions?"

Who knew a simple head nod could be so life changing?

Chapter 7

Jamie

"Will you stop bitching already," I say to Ian, taking a sip of my honey-laced tea. "We're not even recording all day. Sp—"

Shit. I almost used my new nickname for Sammy. No bueno.

I clear my throat to cover my flub. "Sammy has somewhere he has to be later. We're only doing a morning session."

I probably shouldn't be as disappointed about it as I am. I really need to find a hobby or something.

The attraction I've felt since day one is now a full-blown crush after staying out *way* later than intended hanging out with Sammy and his friends.

They are all certifiable, but that is part of their charm. There was a comment here and there about who I am, but the majority of the time they treated me as Jamie the normal guy, not Jamie Hawke the rock star. It was refreshing.

There was not one person I didn't like. I can even admit to being charmed by Maddey. Then again, it's not her fault I'm crushing on her boyfriend.

Unfortunate crush aside, I had more fun with them than with anyone outside of the band. All I want to do is spend more time with Sammy, not less. My brilliant plan backfired in spectacular fashion.

It's a problem. A big, big problem. One with broad shoulders and lickable abs, and dammit, there I go again.

Focus, man.

"Come on, Jame. You know Ian is the cry baby of the band." Andy gives him a playful shove, pulling open the door to the recording studio.

I've been Jame to my friends for longer than I can remember, but after one night I already prefer Sammy's Jam.

"This is true. We're on the back half to thirty. It's time to grow a set, man," Pete adds.

I knock into Pete, he knocks into Andy, and Ian crashes into my back as Steve stops short on the threshold of the studio.

"Well *hello.*" Flirtation drips from Steve's words.

Who the hell is he hitting on? Not Sammy. It may be a secret no one knows, but I know for a *fact* I'm the only one in the band that is strictly-dickly.

"Bro, you can't just *stop* when the rest of us are behind you." Andy curses, pushing past him.

"Sorry, I got distracted." Steve sounds anything but.

"By what?" Ian steps around us all and lets out a surprised "Oh."

Finally through the traffic jam, I see Maddey sitting cross-legged on one of the couches, laptop perched on her lap, Mickey Mouse–printed headphones looped around her neck, black-rimmed glasses perched on her head like a headband. I forgot she asked if she could observe us. She claimed it was for "research."

"Keep it in your pants, boys. This is Maddey, Sammy's girlfriend. Maddey, these delinquents are the rest of the band."

I keep the introductions brief, because if I don't we'll *never* get to work before Sammy needs to leave.

From across the room, Maddey and Sammy share some sort of silent conversation and snort in unison.

"I think I've lost count of the number of times people have thought we were a couple," Maddey says with a wide smile on her face.

Sammy has a similar expression. "And to think I didn't even kiss you. That's usually what gets me in trouble."

"You really *should* learn to not do that so much."

"*Pfft.* Why would I do that? Half the fun of being gay is being able to torture the guys knowing I get to see you girls naked on the reg."

"You're the worst." Maddey giggles.

"You love me." Sammy shrugs.

"For life."

If they say anything else, I miss it because my mind is too busy skipping like a scratched record, trying to make the first part of what was said compute.

Maddey's not his girlfriend?

They're just friends?

He's gay?

What type of alternate *Twilight Zone* universe have I walked into?

"Why do I know you?" Pete's pointing at Maddey, studying her when I tune back in.

"You're gay?" Andy asks, blunt like always.

"Yup." Sammy turns, confidently making eye contact with our guitarist. "But don't worry"—he waves his hand—"you're not my type."

The band loses it in big, loud, leg-slapping guffaws.

Me—I'm reeling.

The guy I find attractive.

The guy I have a crush on.

The first guy I've *liked* probably ever isn't straight like I suspected—he's gay.

Out of the closet gay.

This changes *everything.*

Except…it doesn't.

Because at the end of the day, *I* am very much *in* the closet.

Fuck my life.

Chapter 8

Sammy

Being an out and proud gay man since middle school, I've never shied away from my sexuality being known. I own that shit like a boss.

My family has always treated it like the non-issue it is, and no one, I mean *no one*, has more amazing friends than I do.

So what if I don't "conform" *insert eye roll please* to what stereotypical assholes deem "gay." Who the hell says just because I like dick, I couldn't be a jock? Fuck 'em. Well… probably not because…you know.

I do, however, enjoy the fuck out of the shock value the revelation has on people. Like right now, the guys of BoP are practically rolling on the floor from my easy rejection of Andy.

What I said was true. Andy isn't my type. Jamie though…

Shifting for a better look of the man occupying more of my thoughts than I'd like to admit, I see he's the only one *not* laughing. He looks…well, I'm not sure how he looks.

He's more complicated to figure out than a Rubik's cube— those fuckers are hard.

"I *know* I know you." Pete points to Maddey again once his laughter is under control.

"Isn't the line *haven't I seen you someplace before*?" Ian manages to choke out around his own laughter.

"I'm *not* hitting on her, asshole," Pete tosses back.

"Why not? I would." Steve pushes the drummer aside. "Here, let me if you're not gonna."

"Don't be a dick." Pete shoves back, plopping down next to Maddey.

My best friend looks at me with cartoon character wide eyes. Sure she knew she would meet the band, but knowing it and actually experiencing it are two entirely different things.

"I definitely know you."

"I think I know why he recognizes her." I jump from Jamie's sudden appearance at my side.

"Do tell."

I'm intrigued. But more than that, I like that like last night, we keep falling into these private moments together. Breaking off into our own mini conversations about the others in the room without their knowledge.

"Well..." He braces a tatted arm on the back of my chair, leaning further into my space. "Pete's a *huge* Storm fan, so he might think she's Jordan."

"There's actually another possibility." I give him a look that says *oh do I have a bomb to drop for you*. Given how he thought Madz and I were a couple, he won't be expecting it.

"Tell me." He leans in conspiratorially.

"Remember how I was telling you all the different ways our group is tangled together?"

Jamie nods, and I gotta say, I'm really starting to dig this playful twinkle he's been getting in his eyes lately.

"Maddey dated Ryan for *years*."

"Donnelly?" He shifts back, shocked.

Having met two of Ryan's siblings the night before, the connection of who I meant was easy to make. Plus, we were talking about hockey, and anyone who knows anything even remotely to do with the sport knows who Ryan Donnelly is.

"I'm still having a hard time processing how you never mentioned being friends with so many celebrities."

"Says the man who is the definition of A-list."

I can't help but grin when he blushes.

"How *big* of a Storm fan would you say he is?" My tone turns playful as all kinds of possibilities percolate. I've been staying with Jase for too long because he's starting to rub off on me.

"Oh…only big enough that he *might* want to kick me out of the band when he hears I was hanging out at Jase Donnelly's apartment last night and didn't call him."

"Oh this is gonna be *good,* Jam." I rub my hands together.

"You wanna break it to him, Spins?"

Gah! I feel like a thirteen-year-old girl at a One Direction concert whenever he calls me Spins. It's bad. *So* bad.

"No way. Let her do it. It'll be more fun."

Looks like I'm not the only one content with sitting back and watching the show.

Chapter 9

Sammy

I expected Pete to flip when Maddey told him about our hockey connections, and he did, in big, glorious, now-trending spectacular fashion. It was too good to be missed. Good thing Jamie had the foresight to take video because it was *highly* entertaining.

But this? No way did we see this coming. Who knew attempting to get the band to focus and into the recording booth before Maddey and I had to leave would lead to this?

Maddey is skipping—literally skipping—to the door of the studio. On any given day her excitement levels are high, but now that *all* five members of BoP are gate-crashing her photoshoot, it's like she snorted some of our friend Lyle's specialty espresso beans. I may need to slip her some Benadryl later to calm her down.

This is going to be the furthest thing from productive.

We're already late thanks to the barrage of questions from Pete. We've all been friends for so long I constantly forget how the guys are seen as celebrities to most of the world—massive superstar rockers are apparently not the exception.

"You guys are late," Jordan scolds before her eyes practically pop out of her head when she spots the band filling the room.

We've dubbed her the leader of the group for a reason. She runs one hell of a tight ship, so it's fun to catch her off guard.

"She's right." Now inside, gone is kid-in-a-candy-store-happy Maddey; in her place is bossy-professional Maddey. "Sammy, hair and makeup now. We'll start with Rock and Tuck while you get beautified."

I question my choice of bestie—daily.

Still, we do as we're told, all of us used to being used as models for one thing or another when it comes to Maddey's books.

She greets the photographer she usually uses for her shoots, and I can hear her explaining how the band begged to come when they learned the reason for our shortened recording session was for this.

Maddey may have said I needed beautification, but it only takes the stylist ten minutes to style my hair and give my face a light base of foundation.

Approaching my friends, I can't help but laugh at the middle school dance feel of the room with my friends on one side and the members of BoP on the other. Jamie seems to be the only one floating between the two groups, comfortable having met most of my people last night.

"Hey, babes." I greet all my ladies—with the exception of Jordan because I'd rather *not* have Jake beat me with his hockey stick—with a kiss on the lips and exchange knuckle bumps with the guys.

"I still don't see why you get to kiss the girls and not me." Tucker pouts as soon as the photographer finishes with him and Rocky.

Tucker Hayes doesn't just live up his playboy reputation, he *thrives* on it. He flirts with *any* female within a fifty-foot radius. The only ones immune to his charms—with the exception of Skye for a brief stint in college—are the Covenettes. Hell, the girls call him M-Dubs as a shorthand for man whore.

"Perks of being me, Tuck," I brag to push his buttons.

"Plus, he understands boundaries." Jake Donovan loops an arm around Jordan, pulling his wife against his chest.

"It also helps that we know he's not trying to get into our

pants," Maddey points out, coming over to tug on the hem of my shirt. "Lose this, but careful of your hair."

Gingerly—because you *don't* piss off Maddey McClain—I peel the cotton from my body and drop it on top of her head. Just because you don't piss her off doesn't mean I don't mess with her occasionally.

Her icy blue eyes rake over me from the top of my hair to the tips of my black-and-white Chucks assessingly. "It really is a shame you're gay, Samz."

"Why? You want to run away with me, Madz?"

"Duh."

This has been our running joke for years.

Life would be so much easier for the both of us if I were straight.

We do have a mutual appreciation for sexy half-naked men. So there is that. One of our favorite pastimes is creeping on those who flock to the shore every summer.

"Honestly." The smirk on Skye's face screams trouble.

Oh this is gonna be good.

"I think Tuck is just jealous you aren't kissing him." She blows kisses in Tuck's direction.

"Aww, Tuck. Are you upset you're not my type?" I feign a pout, because what kind of best friend would I be if I didn't play along.

"*Pfft.* You know I'm *everyone's* type, Sammy." Tucker's signature cocky grin overtakes his face. I swear he gets laid from it alone.

"Sorry to burst your bubble, M-Dubs." I drop both my arms around Maddey and Skye's shoulders. "But you are a bit too Abercrombie for my taste."

My gaze shifts to where Jamie is talking with the Donovans. I get a pang in my chest at the sight of the object of my desire—and seriously I've read too many of Maddey's books—standing with the poster couple of our group.

I want what they have. To find my partner, my other half. To know a person so well they become an extension of oneself.

No.

Nope.

Not jealous at all.

Okay. Maybe a little.

"I don't know, Rhodes. I think maybe you're just scared to fall in love with me if you do."

Oh, Tucker.

I can't help but chuckle. He's the biggest shit-stirrer in the group, and that's saying a lot.

"No way, Hayes. You've got that flipped. And *gasp*"—I dramatically put a hand to my chest, clutching my metaphorical pearls—"what a *scandal* it would be if the *great* Tucker Hayes was caught kissing a man."

Chapter 10

Jamie

It turns out Sammy wasn't the only one Maddey enlisted for her photoshoot. Jake Donovan, Ryan Donnelly and Tucker Hayes are also here as models. I can't even *imagine* how much worse the guys would be if Jase was rounding out the group of hockey players.

I don't think I've ever been as entertained in my life as I am right now watching my friends turn into fanboys worthy of an *NSYNC reunion.

I'm riding the high of the day until I'm bitch-slapped with a reality check.

"What a *scandal* it would be if the *great* Tucker Hayes was caught kissing a man."

Sammy's words, though spoken in jest, echo my *deepest* fear. It *would* be a scandal, one of *epic* proportions if I, Jamie Hawke, was caught kissing a man.

Why the hell do I keep daydreaming about us being a couple—an honest-to-god, holding hands in public couple—since learning he swings my way?

I'm fucked in the head, that's why.

"As *entertaining* as it is to listen to you try to convince my best friend to kiss you, M-Dubs—" Maddey pats his chest, with yet another nickname. "—we are here for a reason. And it is *not*"—she holds up a hand to stop Tucker when he tries to speak—"for you to prove that *everyone*, male or female, wants the *great* Tucker Hayes."

The room falls into titters at Maddey schooling the hockey player, but laughing is the *last* thing I feel like doing.

Most of my life I've struggled with being a closeted gay man, one with a very *public* profile, but nothing has compared to the riot of emotions I've been bombarded with since meeting Sammy.

They were tough enough to cope with when I thought he was straight with *zero* chance of anything happening between us. But now? I'm screwed—and not in the fun way.

Boy was I wrong.

The hours since Sammy's sexuality revelation have been torturous. It is one thing to be attracted to a man, hoping not to show it. But it is an entirely different scenario when there's a possibility of something happening—when in reality it shouldn't.

Way to put the cart before the horse, man. Just because the dude likes guys doesn't mean you're *his type.*

See what I mean? Totally certifiable.

"Okay." Maddey claps her hands. "Sammy and Skye, you're up. Go look all smoldery and sexy for the camera so you can help me sell a bajillion books."

They dutifully do what they're told, following the directions given by the photographer, while Maddey moves to stand by my side.

She is one of the nicest, most charming, and genuine people I've come across in a long time. But not gonna lie, I like her just a tiny bit more now knowing she's *not* Sammy's girlfriend.

"You know." She tilts her head so she can meet my eyes. "Now that we're friends, you'll have to be on a cover for me one day. I told you I'm already working on a rock star romance."

"We're friends?" I arch a brow, and she lets out a tinkling laugh.

"Duh." She swats my chest, only illustrating how friendly she feels.

"You spent the night playing Mario Kart with them, right?"

Jake asks over his wife's head. From the way Jordan spoke of him last night, I can tell they are very much in love. Witnessing it in person takes it to a whole new level.

"Yeah."

"He beat Maddey like half a dozen times," Jordan whispers as if giving away state secrets.

"No shit?" The declaration earns me an impressed look from the goalie. "No wonder our phones were blowing up with texts from Vince the moment the plane touched down this morning."

"You guys *really* do take your Mario Kart seriously, huh?"

The night before was an experience unlike any other. Outside the band, there aren't many people I consider *friends*, mostly acquaintances. They made me feel like one of the gang. To hear it confirmed resonates deeply.

"They are *ruthless*," Ryan warns. A part of me is surprised he still models for Maddey with them no longer being a couple, but witnessing how Jase and Rocky had acted last night, it seems the be the standard of their squad. "Word of advice." He points to Maddey. "Careful with this one. She can convince you to do *anything*."

I nod, then everything fades to the background as I take in the scene unfolding before us.

Sammy in all his shirtless glory, has his muscular arms wrapped around Skye's middle like a band. The two are laughing, both their smiles lighting the room, yet his is the only one making me stir behind my zipper.

Like a car wreck, I can't look away. Not even when Sammy bends to nuzzle his face in the crook of Skye's neck, or when I almost crack a molar seeing his lips make contact with the skin on the back of her shoulder.

Those are my lips dammit. They should be on me.

The coppery taste of blood fills my mouth as my thoughts continue to spiral. Biting my tongue probably isn't the wisest way to keep from voicing my objections. My mouth is my instrument and all.

The green-eyed monster beats against my chest wall, a sense of possession washing over me.

I can't keep watching this. I'm already at risk of storming across the room and claiming him as mine.

Talk about outing myself in spectacular fashion.

Feigning a phone call, I bring my phone to my ear and stalk down the back hallway, not stopping until I round the corner into the small kitchenette.

Inside I pace, now knowing what a caged lion feels like.

There's a riot of emotions swirling inside, each one uglier than the last.

Raking my hands through my hair, I yank on the strands until my scalp burns.

I'm a mess.

Where's the Jameson when you need a shot—or ten.

I need to get my shit together ASAP.

"Hey." Sammy's deep voice cuts through the chaos. Who the hell knows how long I've been back here?

Still, I'm startled and whip around to face him standing inside the doorway.

Well, fuck me sideways. He's still shirtless.

The peek I got last night was so short it barely qualified as a glimpse, but that doesn't mean I've been able to forget the sight of his six-pack or the ink on his rib cage. The visual is like a brand on my memory—one I didn't think could have gotten better. Yet it did.

How?

Well…topping the deep v cuts exposed by his slouching jeans, that washboard stomach, and broad AF chest are twin steel bars. Yes, you heard that right, ladies and gentlemen: Sammy Rhodes has his nipples pierced—both of them.

Fuck my life.

"You okay?" His voice is calm, controlled.

Me? I'm slowly losing my mind, nostrils flaring like I'm a goddamn bull getting ready to tear up a china shop.

"Jam?"

The nickname is the last straw. My control snaps.

Not giving one fuck to the consequences, I stalk in his direction, my long legs eating up the space between us with ease.

I cup a hand behind his head, slam him against the wall, and crash my mouth on his.

Chapter 11

Sammy

What in the ever-loving fuck?

I forgot to set my alarm this morning didn't I? Or set it for p.m. on accident because *obviously* I'm still dreaming. It's the only explanation for what is happening right now. Because there's *no* way Jamie-Freaking-Hawke is kissing me.

Right?

Yet…

Can you taste dreams? Is that a thing? Because I swear there's a distinct hint of honey on the tongue stroking mine. You know, like the kind Jamie prefers in his tea.

How is this real life?

Dream or not, when Jamie Hawke kisses you, you kiss back.

My mouth is acting on its own accord; time for the rest of me to get in on the fun.

I wrap my arms around his waist, clutching at the bottom hem of his shirt, the curve of his ass resting just underneath my curled knuckles.

As soon as I respond though, Jamie wrenches himself away, shock written clear across his handsome face.

"*Shit*," he curses, taking another step back. "I'm sorry I did that."

"I'm not." If we're being honest, I've been thinking about

doing that for longer than I want to admit.

Floodgates open—my turn.

Eliminating the micron of space between us with the barest shift of my weight, I tangle my fingers in the longer hair on the back of his head and use my size to move us so he's now the one with his back to the wall.

Unlike his almost violent fusing of our mouths, mine is a gentle melding, tracing the seam of his lips with my tongue until he grants access.

Heart banging against my chest like a kick drum, I'm at risk of wearing the imprint of my zipper on my dick.

I flex my fingers around his head, the new angle causing the scruff of this short beard to scratch along the delicate skin of my lips.

My body trembles.

I like facial hair on my men. I guess it comes from all the time spent around hockey players and their playoff beards.

Tongues stroke.

Teeth nip.

I'm lost.

In the feel, the taste, the smell, every part of me consumed by one thing—Jamie.

Snaking a hand underneath the hem of his shirt, I feel the divots punctuating the top of his spectacular ass, running my fingers around them before reaching to give a squeeze.

The groan that escapes him sounds almost pained. His hips rock forward, and a very obvious bulge presses into my thigh.

I want it.

In my hands, in my mouth—everywhere.

I want nothing more than to pop the button, pull the zipper down, and reach inside to give his cock the appreciation it deserves. To show him I can play the skin flute like a goddamn professional.

We kiss.

And kiss some more.

Praying this moment never ends.

"Tucker!" Skye's shout followed by peals of laughter pierce the bubble and bring us back to reality.

Blowing out a ragged breath, I step back, putting a good foot of distance between us, or else I'll end up kissing him—again.

Jamie's all disheveled hair and swollen lips. It's sexy as fuck. But when I meet his eyes, there's raw fear swimming in those deep purple depths. It slices me to the core.

"Jam." I shift forward but stop when he holds up his hands.

"Don't." His gaze keeps bouncing between me and the hallway, panic pulsing off him in waves. "That shouldn't have happened."

Ouch.

Guilt crashes over me. I'd never come on to a guy who wasn't interested before. Guess there's a first time for everything.

Except...

He kissed *me.*

"I'm sorry, Jam. I thought..."

"No." His hand snaps out to touch my forearm, only to drop as if burned. "It's not that."

His hands go back to his hair, tugging hard enough he looks like he's trying to visualize what he'd look like with a facelift.

"Fuck." He thunks his head against the wall behind him. "I've wanted to do that pretty much from the moment I spotted you inside the conference room." Another thunk. "It's just..." Again he stares down the hallway.

I keep silent, waiting for him to fill in the blanks.

"No one *knows.*" The last word is barely a whisper.

I trust my friends implicitly. If we'd been caught, they wouldn't breathe a word if asked.

But...

"You mean..." The breath whooshes from my lungs, feeling the hit of the realization like a tackle back in my football days.

Did he mean?

No way. He couldn't.

Right?

"What about the band?" I need to know.

"*Sammy*!" Maddey shouts with craptastic timing. "Where you at, dude?" Her voice grows closer with each word spoken.

"Just getting a drink, Tink."

I rush to grab a bottle of water stocked in the fridge and make my way out to catch her before she gets here. Jamie seems like he needs a minute to process.

And Maddey is too observant for her own good. I know there's a risk she'll see the signs on me, but one look at Jamie right now and she would read what just went down like she wrote the scene.

The kissing.

The touching.

The hair pulling.

The nails scratching.

Slow your roll, Rhodes.

The last thing I need is to be sporting a boner when I see my best friend. Maddey and I are close, but not *that* close.

"You good to head out?" I ask casually. The narrowing of her icy blue eyes before they flick between me and the hallway makes me think I wasn't as breezy as I thought.

"Suuurrrre."

Yup, this discussion is far from over.

Chapter 12

From the Group Message Thread of The Coven

QUEEN OF SMUT (Maddey)
Okay Sammy. I've given you hours...
time to spill.

MAKES BOYS CRY (Skye)
Oh yes. The tension in the car earlier was
thick. Give us all the deets.

MOTHER OF DRAGONS (Jordan)
Ooooo. What did we miss?

THE SPIN DOCTOR (Sammy)
Nothing.

QUEEN OF SMUT
Bull. Now come on tell us.

YOU KNOW YOU WANNA (Becky)
Ooooo. Sammy is NEVER in trouble.

YOU KNOW YOU WANNA
This should be good.

YOU KNOW YOU WANNA
*GIF of guy pulling out popcorn and a
drink saying "Ok ok... Go"*

PROTEIN PRINCESS (Gemma)
OMG Beck is really making popcorn
right now *facepalm emoji*

ALPHABET SOUP (Rocky)
Hold on. Time out. Does this have anything to do with a certain rock star that crashed the photoshoot?

MOTHER OF DRAGONS
Oh man. I thought I was the only one picking up on those vibes.

MAKES BOYS CRY
No way. I felt them too.

ALPHABET SOUP
Me too. I didn't think anyone could compete with the pheromones you (Jordan) and Jake give off when you are together... But Holy sexy vibes Batman.

PROTEIN PRINCESS
Why did I have to work? I wanted to come. *Angry faced emoji*

THE SPIN DOCTOR
Aren't the comic references more your brother's forte?

ALPHABET SOUP
Nice distraction attempt, but come on spill the tea.

QUEEN OF SMUT
Oooo, someone's been on a British Royalty kick.

ALPHABET SOUP
What can I say, I've been on an Aven Ellis binge lately.

PROTEIN PRINCESS

Oh I love her books.

YOU KNOW YOU WANNA

Me too. I totally want to be a Modern Royal.

YOU KNOW YOU WANNA:

GIF of girl putting on a crown

MAKES BOYS CRY

GIF of Prince Harry and Meghan Markle

MOTHER OF DRAGONS

Didn't you just say we weren't going to get distracted?

QUEEN OF SMUT

Shit. You're right. Come on Sammy stop holding out on your best friends.

THE SPIN DOCTOR

Fine. But this doesn't leave the group.

PROTEIN PRINCESS

Pinky swear.

MOTHER OF DRAGONS

GIF of a young Dakota Fanning holding out pinky saying "pinky promise"

MAKES BOYS CRY

GIF of Vinny and Pauly D from Jersey Shore doing a pinky promise

YOU KNOW YOU WANNA

BLOOD OATH!!

PROTEIN PRINCESS
GIF of Disney's Genie zipping lips like a zipper

ALPHABET SOUP
GIF of old man from Disney's UP crossing his heart

Chapter 13

Sammy

After hitching a ride back to Jersey to grab a few more things from home before heading back to Jase's place in the city, it really doesn't surprise me that Maddey has now plopped herself in the middle of my bed. After the girls pulled me into another one of their Coven Conversations earlier, I knew it was only a matter of time before my bestie showed up for a more detailed report.

"Madz." I keep folding clothes into my suitcase.

"Samz." She watches me with an expectant grin.

"What's up?" I feign ignorance.

"Don't play dumb. It's not a good look."

Gotta give her points for not pulling any punches. That's Maddey for you.

"I came to figure out where your head's at." The concern I see in her baby blues has me pausing.

"What do you mean?" I move the bag off the bed and sit down beside her.

Her eye scream *don't be stupid,* but she remains quiet, waiting me out, having been taught silence yields more results.

"I'm fine."

"Bullshit." Her dimples flash with the curse. "It's not every day you get kissed by a rock star. There *has* to be a reaction. Especially when that rock star is the same one you've been crushing on hard for the last month."

It's times like these I want to hate her for knowing me so well.

"Tell me about the kiss."

"Why? So it can go in one of your books?"

Guilt stabs me at the flash of hurt that washes over her face.

Shit!

I'm an asshole. There's no reason for me to take out my clusterfuck of emotions on her.

"Sorry." I drop my gaze to my comforter. "That wasn't fair."

"It's okay."

It's not. I give her hand a squeeze, taking the out she's graciously giving me.

"What do you want to know?" I say with a sigh.

"How are you feeling?"

That's the million-dollar question.

"I'm not sure…confused I guess."

She pauses. I appreciate her composing her thoughts instead of bombarding me with questions.

"Okay. Let's start out easy. Do you want it to happen again?"

Duh. How is that even a question? I nod.

"I'm going to assume, since it's not common knowledge, that he's in the closet?"

Another nod.

"Does anyone know?"

I shake my head, and she exhales audibly.

"What about the band?"

Another shake.

"Shit." The curse is whispered, but we're close enough I still hear it. "What are you going to do?"

I look up, not following.

"You've been out forever. Can you really picture yourself being with someone in the closet?"

This time I shrug.

"Well, shit." Maddey flops backward onto the bed.

Good talk.

Chapter 14

Jamie

Twenty-four hours.

That's how much time I allowed myself to stew, debate, curse, and call myself every name in the book.

Not once in the twenty-six years I have been on this earth have I had a slip of control like yesterday.

I kissed Sammy.

I.

Kissed.

Sammy.

In public for fuck's sake.

With the band and a group of relative strangers down the hall.

What the fuck was I thinking?

And as if that wasn't the *dumbest* thing I've ever done, now I'm riding the elevator up to Jase Donnelly's penthouse—again—stoking the flames of potential disaster.

Thank god the Storm are on the road, and only Sammy should be there since he's staying at Jase's for the duration of his contract with BoP.

My hands flex at my sides, and my scowl is visible in the distorted reflection of the stainless-steel doors.

I should just forget yesterday ever happened.

No kiss.

No discovery that Sammy is gay.

That all I need to do is continue to shove my attraction, that fucking *pull*, into the deep corner of my mind.

Yeah. That's it. It's a good plan. A solid plan. Except…

Except now I know what it feels like to have Sammy's lips on mine.

To be held in those built arms.

What he *tasted* like.

I want, no, I *need* more. I can't deny it any longer.

Or how much I genuinely like him.

Ding!

The elevator doors slide open, waiting for me to step through, taunting me.

Pursuing…*something* with him is by far one of the most selfish things I could do. A relationship with me has the potential for more drama and complications than the Kardashians on an episode of *Jerry Springer*. Yet…I *can't* walk away.

The doors start to slide shut, and I throw an arm out before they can close, stepping over the threshold before losing the little bit of nerve I've mustered. It's a dozen steps to the door. All that's left to do is knock.

Well? What are you waiting for, Hawke? He won't know you're here unless you knock.

Why does my subconscious need to remind me that I wasn't announced like last time I was here. Nope, Tobias just waved me along. But that also means I could forget about this, turn around, and leave, without anyone being the wiser.

Man up, Hawke.

Deep breath.

Knock, knock.

Footsteps sound, making their way closer to the door.

Goose bumps break out, and a cold sweat covers my neck.

I swear I'm about to pass out from nerves by the time the door swings open, a shocked-looking Sammy on the other side.

A shirtless Sammy.

In gray sweatpants.

Fuuuuuuck.

Women aren't the only ones who appreciate a pair of gray sweatpants.

The buzz of the electric toothbrush cuts off as he pulls it from his mouth, wiping away any residue with the back of his hand, the move only bringing attention to his delectable lips.

"Do you *ever* wear clothes, Spins?" The question comes out harsher than intended, but I'm distracted.

Hello! Gray sweatpants.

He makes a show of looking down, then looking behind him, a blinding smile on his face when he faces me again.

"Well, shit!" He hits his forehead with his palm, tossing his head back dramatically. "I could have *sworn* I pulled on pants when an unexpected visitor knocked on my door. Guess these are a figment of my imagination." He jiggles the waistband, making the outline of his very impressive package bounce.

I swallow—thickly.

Heat creeps up my neck.

My collar chokes me.

"Did you want to come in?" He swings the door wider. "Or did you plan on staying in the hall all night?'

Chapter 15

Sammy

The intoxicating fresh scent of Jamie's cologne wafts in my direction as he moves past me into the apartment. Since the incident now formally known as *Kiss-Gate*, my thoughts have swung like a pendulum from ball-tightening goodness remembering how his lips felt on mine, to the fear I've cost myself the biggest opportunity of my career.

A general sense of confusion is what I ended up with.

"Let me just grab my shirt—you know, so you don't have to complain about my state of undress." I shoot a smirk over my shoulder, heading for the room I'm staying in.

"It wasn't a complaint."

"*No?*" I stop, arching a brow.

"No. Just a general observation." He pops a shoulder with a playfulness I haven't yet witnessed.

Ducking inside the room, I scoop the faded-from-too-many-washes purple NYU t-shirt from the bed.

The pregame show for the Storm/Lions game plays on the TV but cuts off as a video chat notification flashes across the screen. With our friends spread across the county, our entire squad had the same video chat system installed.

Patting my pockets, I come up empty. Where did I leave my phone? Guess I shouldn't be surprised Maddey is trying to reach me this way.

Except…

Jamie is here.

"I have to answer that or she's just going to keep calling." I point to where a wonky picture of Maddey with bunny ears and whiskers flashes across the flat-screen.

"No worries." Jamie shrugs.

"If you don't want her to know you're here, if you sit in that chair"—I point to one of the massage chairs—"she won't see you."

Folding my lips inward, I debate if I should say anything or not.

"But I can promise you this." I make sure to maintain eye contact so he understands the sincerity of my next words. "She won't breathe a word of this if she knows."

His Adam's apple bobs as he swallows. It's like I can see the pro/con list he's coming up with in his head.

I understand the need for discretion, but in the same breath, I've never been one to keep secrets—at least for long—from my friends. They are just as much my family as my parents.

The call cuts off, only to pop back up a few seconds later.

Jamie chuckles. "You weren't kidding."

"Not even a little bit."

"Go ahead and answer." He waves a hand at the TV.

"You sure?"

He may not realize it, but it's a big step.

"Yeah." With an encouraging smile, he crosses one foot over his knee and settles back against the couch.

Here goes nothing.

"It's about *damn* time," Maddey complains the moment I answer the call.

"Geez, Madz. Take a chill pill, will ya?"

"Don't give me that, Samuel. You said you'd call me when you got back to the city."

"Oh-kay, Mom." Sarcasm drips from my words. To be fair, it's really the only way to handle her.

"Whatever. You know I—" Her eyes go wide. "*Ohhhhh,*

now I get it."

She's spotted Jamie.

"And what *exactly* would that be, Tink?" I play dumb to mess with her.

"You become friends with rock stars and forget all about the little people in your life."

I snort. That might be one of the most ridiculous statements ever.

With professional hockey players, professional fighters, and Maddey herself—multi-time best-selling romance author— I'm sure most of us wouldn't be considered *little people.*

"Was there a point to your phone call besides treating me like I'm a sixteen-year-old who broke curfew and not a twenty-four-year-old responsible adult?"

Jamie coughs in an attempt to cover up a laugh.

"Boo." She pouts. "Fine, whatever. Ruin all my fun, why don't you?"

"Madison," I warn, the use of her full name telling her now is not the time for her usual antics.

"Okay, okay. I was calling to tell you I heard from Con and he'll be home in about a month."

"Anyone else getting leave?" All of Maddey's brothers served as SEALs in the Navy, but depending on their assignments, their time off doesn't always match up.

"No. Just the one pain in the ass to deal with this time. I wasn't sure how long you were contracted to work with the band." Her eyes shift to Jamie, then back to me. "But you know he'll want to get together and stuff."

"My contract is open-ended, but we'll figure something out."

Maddey's family is as much mine as it is hers. There's no way I'm missing an opportunity to see one of the McClain brothers.

"Okay, great. Now you boys have fun. Don't do anything I wouldn't write about." She perks up in her seat, a mischievous gleam I'm well acquainted with lighting her eyes. "Actually *do.*

And take notes. I haven't written a MM book in a while. Give me some inspiration."

Jamie sputters, turning the exact shade of a ripe Jersey tomato.

Subtle my best friend is not. My people may be a steel vault keeping secrets from outsiders, but that doesn't stop them from ragging on those in the know.

I disconnect without saying goodbye, knowing payback's a bitch.

"*Fuck.*" Jamie jumps from the couch, pacing angry circles, pulling at his hair in that way that tells me he's stressed. "You *told* her?"

I could lie and say no. That my best friend is just observant and picked up on the signs—which is true—but I won't start whatever this is on a lie.

"Yes." I hold up a hand to stop the flood I can tell is coming. "But only *after* she asked me about it point-blank."

Violet eyes blink in a wide-eyed stare. The silence is unnerving. I may not know the right words to say, but I refuse to compromise my morals.

"Here's something you need to understand." Needing a physical connection to ground me, I reach to stop his pacing, keeping my hand linked with his as I pull him back to the couch.

"What?" he croaks, yesterday's fear blazing in his eyes.

Fuck, this is harder than I thought.

"I've been friends with Maddey practically my entire life. If there's one person on this earth I could say knows me as well as I know myself, it would be her. I don't think there's *ever* been a time I've been able to keep something from her."

A laugh puffs out as a memory surfaces.

"*Hell*…when I told her I thought I was gay, her exact words were, 'Duh, tell me something I don't know.'"

Chapter 10

Jamie

I listen to the casual way Sammy tells me about coming out to his best friend with awe. And if I'm being honest—a novel concept for me I know—there's also a generous dose of envy too.

Aside from the one man I'd been with—bound by a NDA no less— I haven't told a soul about my sexuality. Not even Pete.

You don't have to say it. I know I'm an asshole.

In my defense, anytime I even *considered* coming out I broke out in a cold sweat, my heart doing its best to beat out of my chest, and the walls always felt like they were closing in on me, the panic is that acute.

I keep waiting for the familiar sensations to hit, but they never come.

Why? Why am I not having a full-blown meltdown? I mean I should be. Maddey knows I'm gay. My secret is officially out.

Where's my freak-out?

Any other time I'd be running from the room, fleeing the penthouse, drowning myself in liquor, and burying my head in the metaphorical sand.

Instead the deep baritone of Sammy's voice washes over me like a soothing balm.

"How—" I clear the emotion choking me. "How old were you?"

"Thirteen. It was the summer before we started eighth grade."

So young.

"Really?"

"Yup." He smiles and tilts his head, causing his hair to flop over his forehead the way I adore.

No longer having to hold back, I give in to the urge and brush it back into place, lingering after.

His hand comes up to wrap around my wrist, the stroke of his thumb on the sensitive skin of the underside of my forearm electric.

"Were—" Another throat clearing. "Were you scared?"

I can't even imagine.

"Of coming out?"

I nod.

"Not to Maddey." It's his turn to pause. "Not to my family either. But Maddey's brothers…that was a *little* intimidating."

"They didn't take it well?"

I'm petrified of how people would react to the news. It holds me back more than the potential fallout to my career. I've been blessed enough to live my dream, singing on stage to sold-out stadiums, but if I lost it, I'd deal. My friends, I can't lose them. I wouldn't survive.

It's a disservice to them, withholding my true self, automatically assuming the worst about their reactions, but I'm a chickenshit.

"They couldn't care less. Connor—the one that will be here next month—I think his words were something about how there'd be less competition with the ladies. He already thought he was a stud at fourteen."

"If you were scared, why come out?"

I need to know.

"It's who I am." He shrugs those delicious shoulders. "Could I have waited? Sure. I probably could have made it all through high school without anyone knowing. God knows Maddey would have been my beard, but I didn't want to live a lie."

He shifts until we're thigh to thigh, shoulder to shoulder, his hand cupping my knee.

"Look." He dips his head to meet my gaze. "I'm not judging you for being in the closet. I told you my story because you asked, not to pressure you into doing the same. I get it, I really do. But I *do* have a question for you?"

So earnest. How am I supposed to deny him? Simple—I can't.

Another nod.

"Does *anyone* know? Your family? The band? Pete?"

I shake my head, and he sighs.

It's embarrassing.

We're such opposites, and not in the good way.

"I…" I look away. "I don't know what it would mean for the band if I came out, but really I'm more scared to lose my friends over it."

"I mean, I can't say anything for certain—I haven't taken *Divination* or anything."

"A *Harry Potter* reference?"

Why am I laughing? How is he able to lighten the heavy?

"We're a group of proud Potterheads. Wait until you meet Lyle. His entire coffeehouse is dedicated to The-One-Who-Lived."

He assumes I'll be around to meet more of his friends? That's a good sign? Right?

"Anyway…based on how they reacted to hearing about me—as in they didn't—I doubt they could give two shits."

Could it really be that easy?

"Can I offer a piece of unsolicited advice?"

Please. Give me all the advice.

"Always."

"Start with one person. Pete maybe. Let him be for you what Maddey was for me."

"Your best friend?"

"Your starting point." He flashes that smirk I'm coming

67

to crave. "Just because what you are revealing feels like this *epic* thing—and I get it, it's not minor—you're altering people's perception of you, but it doesn't *have* to happen in a grand way. Take it one step at a time, one person at a time."

"That's what made it so easy for you?"

He barks out a laugh. "*Easy*? No." The hand on my knee rubs back and forth over the joint. "Just because the people I loved took the news well *doesn't* mean it was easy for me to tell them. I'm pretty sure I felt like I was going to throw up every time. But the relief I felt once I admitted my true self…it was… *freeing*."

God. What would it be like to feel like that?

I've been living under the weight of this secret for so long I've been starting to feel like Atlas trying to hold the world on his shoulders.

The moment swells, growing along with my feelings for him. The way this brave man watches me, no pity, no judgment in his caramel eyes, makes me believe maybe, just maybe, I might be able follow in his footsteps.

I've never really considered coming out. It never seemed like a possibility. Why now? What is it about Sammy that makes me think it isn't just something I should do but something I *need* to?

I launch myself at him, sealing my mouth over his, falling into the kiss and onto the couch.

There is zero hesitation from him. He kisses back just as fiercely, his hands coming to my chest, reversing us until I'm the one with my back to the cushions.

Strong hands grip my face, my legs falling open to allow him to settle fully against me.

Coasting my hands down the breadth of his back, I bunch the material of his shirt until my fingertips skim against the heated silk of skin. I tug until the offending cotton is gone, tossing it carelessly onto the floor.

"Now you *don't* want me to wear clothes?" There's a teasing glint in his eyes as he peers down at me, that flop of hair falling forward.

"If it were up to me, you would never wear clothes. But it's a catch-22 for me." I trail fingertips in a swirl over a shoulder blade, across ribs, until coming to the front and ghosting over one of the steel bars piercing a nipple. "My problem resides in not being able to control myself when faced with all this." I pluck at the bar, causing him to hiss.

He is so much more than just my type. Plus, the raw manliness he exudes turns me on like none other.

Reaching up, I brush the copper strands from his face.

I hold his gaze, saying with my eyes all the things I'm too afraid to admit out loud.

"Kiss me," I whisper.

He obliges without hesitation. Our tongues stroke in a lazy rhythm.

We kiss.

And kiss some more.

He eases away enough to pull my shirt off, and I use the momentum against him to flip our positions again.

I slide to my knees, pushing into the v created by his legs, dropping my mouth to the vein pulsing in his neck. His deep groan is music to my ears.

A suck.

A bite.

The sound of sandpaper fills the room as my stubble drags down his chest.

The contrast of hot skin and cold metal fills my mouth as I wrap my lips around a pierced nipple and suck.

My journey continues, mouth and hands paying homage to the bumps and ridges of his abdomen, tracing the whirls and lines of the DJ headphones tattooed low on his ribs.

I pull back, my hands resting on his spread knees to see a dark spot now staining the front of those damn gray sweatpants.

"Fucking hell, Jam." His voice is like gravel. "Your mouth is almost as good at this as it is singing."

"Sorry to tell you this, Spins." My hands go to the elastic

band of the sweats, curling my fingers underneath it and no further. My experience may be limited to only one other man, but I learned a lot. "But you're wrong in that assessment. Let me show you."

Chapter 17

Sammy

My dick has been letting out a steady stream of precum from the instant Jamie's lips made contact with my body. The feelings rushing through my body are indescribable.

Even with him kneeling in front of me, the sting of beard burn still on my skin, it's hard for me to believe this is real and not a scene from one of Maddey's books.

There's a tug, and I press through my heels, lifting enough so he can yank my sweats down my legs, leaving me completely naked, spread out for his perusal.

The violet of his eyes is a deep eggplant as he rakes his gaze over me so intently it's like a physical caress.

Every hair on my body stands at attention, and my body overheats, waiting to see what will come next.

Another beat.

Another pass over my body.

Another bated breath.

Then Jamie's bending forward, his tongue dragging a circle across the head of my dick, lapping up the precum like it's a melting ice cream cone.

A hiss pushes its way past my teeth at the lazy way he savors my taste. He's barely done anything and this already ranks at the top of my head list.

I'm gripped at the base, then the flat of his tongue licks me from root to tip, my hips surging from the cushion.

Soft lips, prickly hair. Stubble scratches along the underside of my dick as he trails kisses down it for another pass, and I tremble. I'm fucking trembling from the contrasting sensations.

Eyes lift, inky lashes fanning out under dark brows as he lets me see him, no longer hiding. His want is there, plain for me to see. Bending, maintaining eye contact the entire time, he opens his mouth, swallowing the entirety of my dick.

"*Jam.*" More moan than anything else.

A *hmm* of approval.

The suction of his mouth tightens.

"*Fuuuuuck.*"

Up.

Down.

Base.

Tip.

Slowly destroying me with each round trip.

I curve my hands around his shoulders, anchoring myself instead of driving deeper.

Down.

Up.

A brush of lips on my groin.

A relaxed swirl of the tongue.

At the subtlest scrape of teeth, my balls draw tight, release bubbling to the surface. The tether of control snaps, and I fist his hair in my hands, the obsidian strands peeking through my fingers.

"Ja—" I work to swallow. "Jam, I'm close."

"Good," he growls, redoubling his efforts.

There's a tingle at the base of my spine.

Suck.

Pull.

Twist.

More, more, more.

I'm going to come. I'm going to come *harder* than ever

before.

He does this twisting motion with his mouth, and I'm seeing stars, fireworks, even those damn birds Bugs Bunny sees when hit on the head.

"Jam." I grip hard enough I'm sure there will be strands no longer attached to his skull.

"Let me taste you, Spins," he says, only pulling away enough to speak.

How the fuck does a guy say no to that?

They don't.

He grips my hips, demanding I give him what he wants. He swallows around my length, the softness of his throat squeezing like a fist, and that's all she wrote. I come and come some more, coating his golden pipes with every drop of semen I have.

Each pulse of my balls is met with a swallow, not one drop spilling as he greedily drinks me down.

With a final swipe across the too-sensitive head, he rests back on his heels, a satisfied smirk on his handsome face. "Even better than I thought you'd be."

Dead. I'm officially dead.

I'm pretty sure that's the top of my head across the room. Mind officially blown—no pun intended.

My thigh muscles twitch under the patterns he traces on them.

"You doing okay there, big guy?"

I'm the one who just came enough to lose five pounds, but Jamie is the one who seems lighter.

"I'm sorry. Sammy is not home at the moment, please leave a message after the beep."

My joking response is met with melodic laughter. But in all seriousness, I need a minute—or twenty—for proper brain function to resume.

Eyes heavy, I force them open. I don't want to miss a second of the hotness in front of me.

There's no semblance left of the styled faux hawk, and a faint blush shows underneath all the colorful ink decorating his sculpted chest. And fuck me sideways, the smolder he's leveling me with has nothing on the one seen in photos from him performing on stage.

There is *zero* chance that was the first time he's done that. Too bad I can barely function enough to breathe let alone think. I'll contemplate that later. For now, I have much more important things to focus on.

Pushing up, I reach out and haul him to me.

"Now it's my turn."

Absentmindedly I trail the tips of my fingers down the line of Jamie's spine. This was not at all how I expected my night to go. I was supposed to watch some hockey, drink a few beers, maybe continue to tweak Vince's entrance song, then go to bed—alone, not with a shirtless rock star cuddled against me, head on my chest, arm thrown casually over my stomach.

"Can I ask you a personal question?" I need to proceed with caution here.

"We've had our dicks in each other's mouths. I don't think it gets more personal than that."

I let out a bark of laughter at the out-of-character comment.

"Fair enough." I hug him tighter, continuing the up-and-down motion of my hand on him.

"I think I know what you're gonna ask." Jamie's voice is sleepy, content.

"You do?"

He nods, his scruff getting me as he does. "You wanna know if I've been with other men, right?"

It's my turn to nod.

"We had a roadie who would tour with us. I never had to worry about him saying anything because he was required to sign a NDA to work with the band."

Our night may have ended with the highest of highs, but my heart still aches at how isolated Jamie keeps himself—even from those closest to him.

I know I'm one of the lucky ones whose coming out wasn't a horror story, but that doesn't mean it is without it's struggles. There are always going to be ignorant people out there, no matter how far society comes. Having a support system helps quiet the storm.

And what Jamie would face coming out? That will be a fucking hurricane.

Hiding from the band—Pete especially—speaks volumes. I'm out. He's not. Where does this leave us?

"How do you want to handle this?" I'm reluctant to ask but need to. Hiding isn't my style, but the situation isn't as cut-and-dry like mine was.

The short hairs of Jamie's beard set off a fresh wave of lust scratching across my skin as he turns his face to me. Violet eyes bracketed by worry lines meet mine. My hold tightens, protective instincts flaring.

Was this how Jake felt when he and Jordan dated on the DL during college? Like he was being ripped in two? Wanting to shout his feelings from the rooftops, only to be handcuffed by their secret?

"I—" Jamie looks down.

"It—" He starts again only to stop.

A puff of air blows across my nipple when his words cut off for the third time.

"I know it makes me the most selfish person ever to ask this…"

"Jam," I encourage, running a thumb along his tense jaw. Again his eyes lower.

"Can we… Can we keep this between us for now?"

The voice in my head says no—it goes against how I've lived my life since I was a teenager—but the one in my heart is louder.

"Yes."

"*Really*?"

"Really." I push onto an elbow. "But you need to know…"

I pause, not sure how he'll react. "My girls know. There's no keeping secrets from The Coven. They are too good at sussing out information."

"You said you trust them though, *right*?" Anxiety drips off him.

"With my life." There's nothing but conviction in my words.

"Then I trust them too."

It will be a delicate balance, walking the line with those who know and those still in the dark, but we can manage—for a while at least.

Chapter 18

Jamie

The guys are at my place, taking over my living room like it's their own. Though to be fair, we all do it.

"This is bullshit." Pete throws his hands in the air after I take first place in another round of Mario Kart. "Since when are you *this* good?"

Rolling my lips in, I attempt to hold in a grin and fail.

"Oh, shit." Ian sits up on his knees, getting into optimal position to stir up trouble. "Has *someone* been playing without us?" He tuts his finger side to side. "What a naughty bird."

The rest of us groan. Ian thinks he's so punny.

"And *I* think you assholes just need to learn how to lose like men," Andy counters.

"Truth." Steve taps his beer against Andy's.

"Besides—" Andy turns to Ian. "—Pete is the only one who can bitch. We all know you have the worst record in the entire band."

"Burn." Pete mimes dropping a bomb and making it explode.

My phone vibrates in my pocket, and I'm far enough away from the others to answer without any Nosey Nellys looking over my shoulder.

THE SPIN DOCTOR: Next time I need you to remind me NOT to give in to peer pressure.

I can't help it—I laugh, waving off Pete when he looks over to see what's up.

Is it wrong that I'm taking enjoyment from his pain?

From the stories I've heard and the Coven Conversations I've read over his shoulder lying in bed, I can only imagine what they are getting into at the Blizzards game.

ROCKSTAR MAN: Umm…

ROCKSTAR MAN: *GIF of Octavia Spencer saying "Don't be a loser. Just do it"*

THE SPIN DOCTOR: Ouch, babe. That hurts. You're siding with the Covenettes?

I adore how easily he calls me babe. I don't get to hear it—or my all-time fave, Jam—during the day, but when we're alone, or in text, he never shies away.

ROCKSTAR MAN: I should probably point out two things.

ROCKSTAR MAN: 1. They are YOUR friends

ROCKSTAR MAN: 2. YOU are an honorary member of their little group. So shouldn't you be used to it by now?

THE SPIN DOCTOR: Oh someone has jokes I see. Just you wait. One day they are going to be dragging your sexy AF ass out with us and you'll see.

I want to be a part of the craziness. This last month has been both the best and the worst of my life.

The Covenettes weren't the only ones Sammy told about our relationship—Jase knows too. There was no way to avoid that one, seeing as Sammy is living with him while he works with the band.

We haven't told Pete about those living arrangements—if we did we wouldn't have anywhere free to be a couple—but we did arrange an introduction after a Storm game. He epically and embarrassingly lost his shit.

Ian filmed it.

Andy posted it.

Jordan texted me thanking us for almost breaking the internet.

ROCKSTAR MAN: I'm pretty sure they torture me enough whenever we hang out with them.

THE SPIN DOCTOR: Puh-lease. They haven't even BEGUN to hit you with the good stuff. You're still in the training wheels stage. Talk to me when they come off. Then we'll see if you'll still want to date me.

I can't think of *anything* that would make me want to *not* date Sammy anymore. Unfortunately, I doubt he could say the same thing about me.

He may not have said anything, but I've noticed the way his hand flexes when we can't touch in public or how his jaw clenches when female fans get too handsy.

Looking around the room, I wish for the courage to admit the truth.

But more than anything, I want to be brave like Sammy and stop hiding.

What's scarier though?

Coming out isn't what scares me most anymore.

Losing Sammy is.

Chapter 19

Jamie

I can't believe we only have one song left." Pete leads us out of the booth.

Three months of Sammy working as our producer—two of those spent as my secret boyfriend—and the album I thought would never come to fruition is about to be complete.

Every time we spend time with Sammy's friends, it adds to my hope that I can do this. That this can be my reality and not just from behind closed doors.

But…it also adds to the guilt.

I look around the studio, each of my bandmates spread out on the various furniture, talking, joking, and generally having a good time, including Sammy as if he has always been a part of us, all while completely unaware of how significant of an addition he has become.

Fuck.

I love him.

I'm in love.

And that isn't the scary part. Nope, the scary part is I can't hide it or who I truly am any longer. It's time to come clean with my people.

Like Harry Potter, I don't belong in the closet.

Who knew what this could mean for me? Could it cost me my career? My band? My friends?

"Ooo, Samz, it's a good thing you don't have a boyfriend

because he might get all sorts of jealous." Andy's looking down at something on his phone, and I'm hit with a sense of foreboding.

"What? Did you just declare your undying love for me on Twitter or something?" Sammy sends me a discreet look over his shoulder before returning his attention to Andy.

"No." He snorts. "But maybe I should, just to stir the pot after this garbage."

"Why are you always such a cryptic asshole? Just spit it out already," Pete complains.

"Well…looks like the Twitterverse is all in a tizzy, saying these two"—he points to both Sammy and me—"are in some sort of secret relationship."

The bottom falls out of my stomach. How could this be? Did someone see me leaving Jase's place one of the nights I stayed with Sammy?

My mind goes blank, and the room around me goes fuzzy.

The phone gets passed around the group, and I'm not brought back to reality until it makes its way to me, a picture from two nights ago when we all went to see the Storm play on the screen. Sammy and I are high-fiving, celebrating the goal Jase had scored. The picture itself is innocent enough. What would make someone think we were a couple? We weren't doing anything coupley.

When I lift my head, Sammy's watching me expectantly.

This is my chance.

My opening to come clean.

It's practically being served up on a platter.

Except…

I can't.

I see the moment Sammy realizes my decision. The light in his caramel eyes dims until the irises are almost brown.

My boyfriend is slipping away, and instead of grabbing on with both hands, I do…nothing.

81

Chapter 20

Sammy

I wait for Jamie to say something—*anything*. Hiding our relationship is getting old. I've told myself I could deal. I mean, what was the alternative? Not having Jamie? Yeah, no, I didn't want that.

That was before this. Another idiot hiding behind the internet, trying to start rumors because of my sexuality. I'm no stranger to it. People love drama, and having multiple famous associations in my life, the more aggressive trolls like to try and use me as a way to "out" the others for click bait. I've lost count of the number of times the media tried to link me and Jase romantically because I stay at his place often.

Looks like they finally got it right. I am with Jamie. We are dating, and every day the strength of my feelings grows.

Day by day I've watched as Jamie inched closer to coming out to his friends.

Except now…

Nothing.

It's like I can see him not just pull the door shut on his closet, but locking it for good measure.

I thought I could do it. That I was strong enough for the both of us.

Was I wrong?

I hate how it feels like I'm living a lie.

Is love supposed to hurt like this?

Love?

Wait…

Do I love him?

Shit! I think I do.

I wish Jamie was in a place where he could take this and use it to launch our relationship out into the world, but it would be unfair for me to ask.

Space. That's what I need. Somewhere without prying eyes to wallow and beat myself up over my selfish desires and get my head on straight.

Okay, okay. Time to leave. I need to take some time to myself before I do something I can't walk away from.

Calmly, casually, I push from my chair.

"Eh, don't worry about it. It'll blow over," I say to Jamie, giving him the weakest and least reassuring smile ever, and walk out of the room.

Chapter 21

Jamie

I clutch the tumbler of Jameson so hard I'm surprised the glass doesn't shatter while I pace my apartment. No matter how much liquor I drink or how many steps I take, nothing helps fill the hole gouged in my chest.

I've had a front-row seat to Sammy's struggle over keeping our relationship a secret, but the way he looked when he left the studio earlier was on another level. He looked...broken.

I did that to him. I took one of the happiest men I have ever met and blackened part of his spirit.

Me and my goddamn cowardliness.

Why the fuck couldn't I just tell my friends the truth? What is so *goddamn* hard about saying, "Hey guys, I'm gay."

But did I do it?

Nope.

Instead I was a chickenshit.

He has no idea how much he means to me.

That changes today.

No more hiding.

I need to do it now.

I can't do this on my own.

I need reinforcements.

ROCKSTAR MAN: I need help.

QUEEN OF SMUT: Of the professional variety? Because I'm not sure I qualify.

ROCKSTAR MAN: Are you always this much of a smartass?

QUEEN OF SMUT: My gift is my curse.

ROCKSTAR MAN: Look…I've witnessed multiple Coven Conversations, and while I adore you ladies, now is not the time for your squirrel brain.

QUEEN OF SMUT: *squirrel emoji*

ROCKSTAR MAN: Can you please be serious so I can tell your best friend I love him?

QUEEN OF SMUT: Well shit. Hold please.

From the Group Message Thread of The Coven

QUEEN OF SMUT
Ok, listen up ladies. We have a rock star in need of assistance.

MOTHER OF DRAGONS
Does this have anything to do with Sammy being a Debbie Downer all night?

MAKES BOYS CRY
He's a guy, wouldn't the correct term be something like Dudley Downer?

YOU KNOW YOU WANNA
Unless he goes drag and he's Dixie Downer.

YOU KNOW YOU WANNA

OMG!

YOU KNOW YOU WANNA

Madz, do you think we can convince
Sammy to do drag?

ALPHABET SOUP

GIF of RuPaul gasping

PROTEIN PRINCESS

*GIF of RuPaul in full drag saying
"I can't wait to see how this turns out"
holding up a pair of binoculars*

MAKES BOYS CRY

GIF of girl pointing up saying "This"

YOU KNOW YOU WANNA

Oh I remember that episode of
RuPaul's Drag Race.

ALPHABET SOUP

I love that show.

PROTEIN PRINCESS

Me too.

YOU KNOW YOU WANNA

I'm jelly of their contour skills

MAKES BOYS CRY

GIF of girl saying, "Girl Same."

YOU KNOW YOU WANNA

BLOOD OATH!!

ROCKSTAR MAN

Wow you guys REALLY don't EVER stay on topic, do you?

MOTHER OF DRAGONS

I thought you wanted our help with something?

ROCKSTAR MAN

I'm sorry. I bow down to your greatness.

ROCKSTAR MAN

GIF of Garth and Wayne in Wayne's World bowing saying, "We're not worthy"

MAKES BOYS CRY

Seems a little overboard, but I'll never say no to a man bowing down.
<<Check the text handle.
Crying laughing emoji

QUEEN OF SMUT

Okay, okay...let's stop before we make Jamie change his mind about telling Sammy he loves him.

MAKES BOYS CRY

Oh shit! *Shocked faced emoji*

YOU KNOW YOU WANNA

Gemma we need popcorn.

ROCKSTAR MAN

Can you help or not?

QUEEN OF SMUT

Yup. Get your ass to the Garden right now.

ROCKSTAR MAN

??

QUEEN OF SMUT

The Storm are playing. We are here.

MOTHER OF DRAGONS

I'll have a ticket waiting for you and an attendant will take you to a private box. Hurry up. The 3rd period is about to start. We aren't going to be here much longer.

Not even hot guys in hockey gear are enough to distract me from the ache in my heart.

I haven't heard from Jamie since I left the studio earlier, and I can admit I haven't been the best company because of it.

"You know." Connor leans in to be heard over the cheering crowd. "I always thought Ryan was exaggerating when we'd hear stories of The Coven on our video chats, but seeing them in action was something else."

Having the youngest McClain brother here has been a nice distraction. Plus its always entertaining to witness someone being given The Coven Experience.

"Jase and Vince knew what they were doing when they named them," I agree.

"Hell yeah. I swear they were more efficient in their planning than some of my missions."

"You've been spending too much time around Jase because you're starting to exaggerate like him."

"There are worse things." He tips his beer to me.

The smack of bodies hitting the boards in front of us brings our attention back to the game. Callahan lines up for a face-off in the Storm zone, my mind drifting from the game back to what I'm supposed to do about Jamie.

I should have taken Maddey's concerns more seriously. I'm

not sure how much longer I can keep doing this. It hurts.

"Hey, Sammy." Jordan turns in her seat to face me. "I know this isn't the best timing, but the Garden's musical director was wondering if he could talk to you about possibly revamping the Storm's goal song."

"Now?"

"Yeah. He's upstairs in one of the boxes. Do you mind?"

Why does she look like she expects me to say no? I've never been able to deny my girls anything. Why would I start now?

"If you're okay missing some of the game, who am I to say no?"

We make our way out of our rows, and I grin at the maternity shirt of two babies in hockey gear facing off.

The trip to the suite level is quick, and I follow her to one of the executive suites.

"Jor?" I ask when she doesn't move to enter.

"Just remember we love you."

Because that wasn't cryptic as fuck or anything.

"Oh-kay?"

"Go ahead." She thrusts her chin at the door.

"Aren't you coming?"

"No. Call me if you need us," she calls over her shoulder, already walking away.

Okay, that was odd.

What do I do here?

Do I just walk in?

Do I knock?

Fuck it. He's expecting me. I push the heavy wood door open and step inside.

I move my gaze from left to right, looking for the music director.

Only the music director isn't the one waiting for me—Jamie is.

Chapter 23

Jamie

I'm back to pacing, only this time it's at the Garden instead of my apartment. How Jordan was able to acquire an empty suite during a game I have no idea, but even I have learned not to question The Coven.

The buzz I worked hard for faded with the mad dash to get here in time. With less than five minutes of the game, the Storm up 2-1, my reason for coming still hasn't shown.

Was this a mistake?

No.

The mistake was allowing *anything* to put that defeated look in my boyfriend's eyes. Never again will I be the catalyst for it.

By the time the door pushes open, I'm about ready to crawl out of my skin I'm so fucking anxious.

I purposely only turned on one set of lights so I can see him but he can't see me. I use the opportunity to study him and the forlorn expression on his face. Gone is the beaming smile I fell for.

I did that. This is all my fault.

"Jamie," he rasps.

Jamie. Not Jam.

Fuck.

"Spins—"

"Don't." He slashes a hand through the air. "Don't taint it with the ugly I'm feeling."

I reach out a hand, curling it around the bicep I rested my head against the night before.

"I'm sorry," I say simply—honestly.

"I know." He blows out a breath. "And I'm sorry too."

My head snaps up. There's no way I heard him correctly. "You are?"

"Yes. I am." His head falls forward, and so does that flop of hair. I reach to brush it away, but he backs away from my touch and my heart sinks.

"This is as much my fault as it is yours."

"How?" My voice breaks, afraid of the answer.

"I shouldn't have agreed to do this while it needed to remain a secret. It's not who I am. But I was selfish. I wanted you too much and ignored all my internal alarm bells."

He sucks in a lungful of air, and my gaze drops to watch how his chest expands.

"It doesn't help that I feel like I'm warring with myself. I want to be able to touch you without having to worry about what it could make people think. But I know how selfish that is."

That's what I want too. We could have been doing that all along if it weren't for me.

"I may not agree with your reasons for staying in the closet, but I would *never* pressure you to come out. I just…" His voice cracks as he lets the sentence trail off.

"You just what?"

"I just don't know if I can keep living a lie, even if I love you."

"You love me?" I squeak.

"Are you seriously asking me that right now?" He arches a brow. "Of course I love you. Why do you think this hurts so much? I want to be able to be with you outside of Jase's apartment. I hate that it's so easy for you to turn us off when we're in public."

"You think that's *easy* for me?" God. It has been the

hardest thing I've ever had to do.

"It doesn't matter, Jamie."

If he calls me Jamie *one* more time, I'm going to fucking lose it.

I'm *Jam*, his Jam. And he is my fucking Spins.

Fuck this.

Fisting the front of his shirt, I spin and all but slam him into the wall, my mouth on his.

There's a thud.

A grunt.

A groan.

Tongues lash.

Hair is pulled.

Every sound combining into the most beautiful melody I've ever written.

A love song for the ages.

An epic ballad.

It isn't until my lungs *scream* for oxygen that I pull away, cradling his head in my hands, resting my forehead to his.

"I love you, Spins. I love you so much it scares me. But even the thought of losing you *petrifies* me. Any fear of what coming out will do to my life *pales* in comparison to what a life without you will do to me."

"Jam."

There it is.

"I'll go out there"—I thrust an arm toward the rink—"and tell the whole world, *I*, Jamie Hawke, love *you*, Sammy Rhodes. And I don't give *one* fuck what they think about the fact you are a man. I. Love. You."

He mirrors my hold, his fingers interlocking at the back of my skull. "Tomorrow."

"Tomorrow?"

"You can tell the world you love me tomorrow. Tonight is for us."

Tonight and every night after.

•

Chapter 24

Jamie

The door to the apartment slams with a bang, the restraint needed leaving The Garden and on the cab ride back snapping, and we're on each other.

"What about Jase?" I mumble between kisses.

"He'll go out with the girls." My leather jacket is shoved from my shoulders.

"We should have gone back to my place." His jacket goes, and I'm already working on his shirt.

"Too far."

We stumble our way down the hall to the guest room, a trail of clothes left behind like breadcrumbs on the way.

Not taking any chances, I kick the door shut with my heel and click the lock home. I'll be damned if anyone is interrupting this.

Need pulses in my blood, and I take a moment just to stare at the man in front of me.

Fuck I have good taste.

Sammy's copper hair is all kinds of disheveled, his broad chest heaving, the light glinting off the silver rods piercing his nipples. The black ink on his side only highlights the cut of muscles leading to the deep v bracketing his groin.

He keeps those melted caramel eyes locked on mine as he shoves his boxer briefs down his strong legs and kicks them to the side.

"Why is it you're always the one overdressed in this relationship, Jam?"

Looking down, I realize he's right. My hands stilled at the button of my fly, but I was a little bit lost at the sight of my hot AF boyfriend. Could you blame me? I mean really, Sammy is *all* man, and he's all mine.

"It's not my fault you have a problem keeping your clothes on." I get to work until we're both naked and at attention.

"You say that like you're complaining."

"No." I close the distance between us, my hands skimming up the plain of his chest, thumbing the piercings along the way. "Well…maybe I was initially. It made it *supremely* difficult to keep my hands off of you."

"The only thing I see wrong with that is that your hands *weren't* on me." His hand snakes around my hips, pulling until we're chest to chest. A groan escapes as the head of my dick brushes the solid muscle of his thigh.

"It was a *problem* because I was hiding. No more." Another flick of the piercings. "Now." A squeeze of the pecs. "I get to touch you." My hands roam down, tracing each bump of his abdominals. "*All* I want." Down into his v cuts. "*Wherever* we are."

"*God* yes."

We both groan as his dick leaves a trail of pre-cum underneath my navel, both of us painfully hard.

"I need you," I growl.

"I'm yours."

The automatic, easy acceptance is all I need. Pushing forward, I kneel on the edge of the mattress as he sinks onto it. Our mouths stay fused together as I follow down until I'm stretched out on top of him.

His fingers thread into my hair as I blaze a trail of kisses down his body.

Lips.

Jaw.

Down the line of his neck

Teeth scraping the bump of his collarbone.

One nipple ring, then the other.

One, two, three, four, five, six abdominal muscles.

Down the v cut.

Mouth open wide, I take the entirety of his length.

He groans and I feel a painful, but pleasurable, tug on my hair as I work him over.

Up.

Down.

I lick the vein running along the underside before swirling around the head again.

"Jam."

I release him and kiss back up his chiseled body, balancing on my elbows and caging him between them.

Emotion swells in me like a crescendo.

"I love you, Spins."

Chapter 25

Sammy

"I love you, Spins."

Those are officially my four favorite words in the English language when strung together.

I still can't believe I'm hearing them.

I trace lazy figure eights on Jamie's jaw with my thumb, the short scruff emitting a faint sandpapery sound.

Something new swims in the deep purple pools of his eyes. Yes, there is love, but also more. I can't quantify it, but I feel it. It flows out, harmonizing with my heart.

This is it. *Jamie* is it for me. He is my person, and yes, there will still be hurdles to come, but we will manage them—together.

I push up, flipping our position so I'm now hovering over him.

"I love you too, Jam. So *fucking* much."

I'm yanked down for another kiss, my lips, chin, cheeks all feeling the scratch of his beard. I'll have wicked beard burn come morning, but I couldn't care less if I tried.

"I need you, Spins." Legs wrap around my hips.

"You have me." I cradle his face in my hands, thumbs resting on his temples. "I'm not going anywhere."

"I *can't* wait anymore. Take me now."

Not having to be told twice, I shift, arm stretching for the nightstand. My hand closes over the bottle of lube, scooping it and a foil wrapper out of the drawer.

Easing one of Jamie's legs from where it's wrapped around me, I thumb open the top and squirt a generous amount of the cool liquid onto my fingers.

I stroke the sensitive skin of his taint, and he shudders under the caress. I slip a finger past the tight ring of his ass. The way he clutches my shoulders is urgent, but I keep my movements unhurried.

I slide my finger in and out in a lazy rhythm, adding a second, then a third as he opens for me.

"Spins." He chokes out a moan. "Stop teasing me. Fuck me. Now."

I reach for the condom, opening the wrapper with my teeth, sucking in a breath as the latex rolls down my aching dick.

My molars snap together as I coat my length with lube, so keyed up I'm not going to last much longer.

I position myself at his entrance, and our eyes remain locked, not blinking once as I push inside, inch by slow inch.

His hands wrap around my wrists bracketing his face, holding on. I pull my hips back, then push forward.

In.

Out.

The wetness on my stomach grows as his cock continues to leak pre-cum trapped between our bodies, rubbing with each roll of my hips.

I flip a hand over, linking our fingers together.

"Oh, god." He moans when I hit his prostate. "*Fuuuuck.*"

And again.

Sweat trails down my spine in an effort to hold back my orgasm.

He clutches me.

I pick up speed, my rhythm a pounding beat.

"Sammy," he roars as he comes, soaking my belly.

Two more pumps and I'm spilling inside the condom.

My arms give out, and I roll to the side to avoid crushing

him.

Our arms loop around each other's necks like we're slow dancing at middle school dance.

"Hi." He fingers the hair on the back of my head, setting off pleasant tingles with the intimate touch.

"Hi."

I can *feel* how goofy my smile is. The power of a mind-blowing orgasm can do that to a person.

"Thank you," he whispers.

"For making you come?"

I don't know if I've ever been thanked for sex before.

"No."

"*No?*" I feign offense

"Don't be an ass. You know it was good for you too."

"*Good?*" I rear back. "I think you need to spend some time with Maddey so you can learn some new adjectives because that was so much better than *good.*"

"Such a smartass."

"I know." I pull back to take care of the condom, tying it off and dropping it into the garbage beside the bed. "But then again, you've met The Coven—I have to keep up."

"True."

He laughs, then sobers.

"But seriously…thank you…for not giving up on me." He holds up a hand when I try to cut in. "I love you, Sammy Rhodes, and it's time the rest of the world knew it."

Chapter 20

Sammy

Buzz.
Ping.
Buzz.
Ping.

I throw an arm out to stop the incessant buzzing, but as I hit the button on my phone, the sound continues. In the distance I hear *Yoshi* over and over as someone blows up Jase's phone.

All three phones going off can't be a good thing, and I really should see what's up, but then the scruff from Jamie's beard brushes against my bare back, and checking text messages becomes the last thing I want to do.

His arm wraps around my waist, and I roll so my back is flush with his front. Scruffy kisses trail between my shoulder blades, the moment almost perfect except for the incessant ping and buzz of our phones.

Two quick knocks are our only warning before the door pushes open—damn us for not locking it after grabbing a midnight snack—my sarcastic comment dying on my tongue when I catch the look of raw panic on Jase's face.

I jerk to sit up. If Jase, Mr. Laidback-Good-Time-Boy isn't smiling, something has to be seriously wrong. The phone in his hand continues to call out *Yoshi*, but he remains silent.

"Jase?" I ask, Jamie sitting up beside me.

Ping.

Buzz.

Yoshi.

"Ummm…" He looks down at his phone, then back to us.

"Jase?" I try again, but no response. A trickle of unease sets in.

Is someone hurt? Did someone die? Is that why our phones are going off?

No. That doesn't make sense. If that were the case, Jamie's phone wouldn't be blowing up.

"What's going on?" I make one last attempt, still not reaching for my phone.

Ping.

Buzz.

Yoshi.

"Have you checked your phone at all this morning?" Jase directs his question to Jamie.

"No. I was ignoring it in favor of trying to get it on with my boyfriend, but then you came barreling in here," Jamie answers.

"Oh, I'm *sorry*, Your Royal Rockness." Jase bows. "It's so *rude* of me to enter a room in my own house."

There's the Jase Donnelly we know and love.

Ping.

Buzz.

Yoshi.

"Are you ever gonna tell us what's up with the wake-up call?" I try to bring the conversation back around.

"Check your phone." Again he speaks to Jamie.

"Jase," I warn, a sense of dread settling over me like a weighted blanket.

"Just do it. Both of you."

There are more than two hundred text notifications on my phone. It's a Coven Conversation on steroids, except the girls aren't the only one texting, the guys are too.

"Tell me no one's dead." I whip my gaze up to Jase, scrambling out of bed.

"Not yet," he says ominously.

"Spins." Jamie's voice breaks, and he's doing his best impression of Casper with his pale pallor.

"Jam?" I'm at his side in an instant, the mattress bouncing underneath me. "What's wrong? What happened?"

"We—I've—They—"

With each word that cuts off, my anxiety grows.

Ping.

Buzz.

Yoshi.

"Jam? Talk to me, babe." I run a hand in soothing circles up and down the line of his spine. Under my touch he vibrates more than his phone.

"Someone—" A pause. "Someone saw us." His voice is barely a whisper as he shows me the latest article from *TMZ*. On the screen is a grainy picture of us kissing.

"Look—" I take the phone, but the sound of the front door slamming followed by footsteps storming down the hall stops me from continuing. Whoever is here is *pissed*.

I arch a brow at Jase, but he only shrugs to say *I have no idea*.

We don't have to wait long. Seconds later the other half of the Donnelly twin set enters the room, and a furious-looking Jordan stops beside her brother.

It takes a lot to flip Jordan's switch and invoke the mother of dragons side of her that earned her text handle. Right now though? She is next-level angry, at least if the way she looks like she was about to breathe fire is any indication.

"When I find the person who sold you two out to the trash rags, I am going to *murder* them." The word murder comes out in a slight growl.

"I don't think you'd hold up in prison, JD." Jase drops an arm around her shoulder.

"I'd have to be caught first."

Gone is my bestie; in her place is the badass PR dynamo she has become.

I've never been more grateful to be considered one of her own.

Chapter 27

Jamie

Leaning against the counter, cradling a mug of coffee in my hands, I look over the war room the place has transformed into, barely recognizing Jase's apartment an hour later.

It wasn't long after Jordan showed up that the rest of the Covenettes arrived, each of them acting like knights ready to go into battle.

The chaos inside the apartment is reminiscent of backstage before one of our shows. People are everywhere, not one person is sitting as they all but run from one task to another, all while a chorus of cell phones provide the soundtrack to the morning.

My phone is the only one going unanswered at the moment. I can't deal. The dread over what the band must think is a lead ball in my stomach. All my plans to tell them gone with one picture.

But the longer I watch how the people who love my boyfriend most rally around not just him but both of us, realization hits me like a spotlight.

What the hell am I so scared of? Why wouldn't I tell the band? Coming out won't change who I am. I'll still be the same Jamie Hawke they always knew.

And who knows, maybe I'll be an even better version of myself not having to hide a piece of myself.

Decision made, I turn for the bedroom to retrieve my phone and thumb open Pete's contact.

"About *fucking* time, asshole," Pete snarls, answering after barely a ring.

"Sorry." And I am, both sorry and an asshole. "Listen…I need to talk to you and the rest of the band." Among other people.

"You're damn fucking right you do."

"I'm not sure where will be best, bu—"

"Here works."

I'm about to ask where when I realize his voice didn't come from the phone but by the door. I whip around to find him leaning against the doorjamb.

"How?"

"How did I know where to find you?"

I can't see thanks to the Storm hat pulled low on his head, but I'm sure his right eyebrow is raised.

"Yeah."

"I used our friend finder app."

Emotion strangles me.

"Look, Pete—"

"Not the time, bro. I was told we were needed out there"— he hooks a thumb behind him—"right now. That Jordan doesn't seem like the type of person I want to piss off, so the rest can wait."

I think of when she first showed up, a grin tugging at the corner of my mouth.

"I also may have been threatened within an inch of my life by Maddey. I swear for a girl who is barely five feet tall, she's intimidating as fuck."

I agree with the assessment, hit once again by how much Sammy's squad has accepted me into the fold. I can only hope the band being here means they could do the same.

"You good, Jam?" Sammy asks, when we rejoin the chaos.

"I'm good, Spins." I go to him without any hesitation, taking comfort when the back of his hand brushes mine.

"God, you two make me sick," Connor says.

"The fuck?" Pete roars.

"Are you serious right now?" Andy moves to Pete's side.

"You wanna try that again?" Steve and Ian close ranks.

They are...defending me?

This is *nothing* like how I expected the first interaction with them to go.

"Don't be an idiot, Con." Maddey steps into the fray, ignoring the scowling rockers behind her to smack her brother upside the head.

"What?" Connor asks, then reads the room. "Oh shit."

"Oh good. Did you just play it back in your head?" Maddey rolls her eyes. "And to think...they entrust you with classified information."

"Yeah, no." Connor holds his hands up in surrender. "I didn't mean it like *that*."

"Oh yeah? Then *please* tell us what you meant before I lay you out for gay bashing my best friend." Pete is in full intimidation mode.

Sammy squeezes my hand, and we snicker at the ridiculousness happening in front of us. It doesn't matter how much Pete acts like a "tough" rocker, I'm pretty sure Connor is trained in how to kill a person with his pinky.

Through all the macho posturing, the thing that resonates is the band coming to my defense. They don't need to. Connor isn't a threat—hell, he couldn't be more supportive if he tried.

"What I was trying to say—" Connor walks to Jordan, dropping an arm around her shoulders. "—is that even this one and her husband—the most in love, sickly sweet couple of all time—don't even have pet names for each other. But you two are all Spins and Jam up in here."

"Sounds like *someone's* jealous they don't have a nickname," Skye calls out, then returns to her phone call.

Maddey snorts.

Jordan giggles.

Sammy barks out a laugh.

"Don't worry, Con. You'll always be my second favorite McClain. Even if you don't have a nickname," Sammy coos.

"Second favorite?" Connor scoffed.

"Duh." Maddey pats him on the chest.

"While I'm all for putting our brothers in their place." Jordan pushes out of Connor's hold. "We have more important things to discuss right now."

Again, the mood shifts.

I meet the eyes of the brothers of my heart. Time to do what I should have *years* ago.

Chapter 28

Sammy

It took everything in me to sit back and allow Jamie to face this on his own. He isn't alone *alone*—my hand holds his, lending my strength should he need it.

"Guess I should start off by apologizing," Jamie says, taking a moment to look each of his bandmates in the eye.

"You mean for not telling me you've been pseudo-living with Jase Donnelly?" Pete deadpans.

"Keeping me from my fans, Jame?" Jase swaggers over.

"Dude? Read the room, wombmate." Jordan's already shaking her head at her twin.

"Pete," Jamie tries again.

"Stop." Pete holds up a hand. "That's the only thing you would need to apologize for."

"But—"

"Nope." Again Pete cuts him off.

"But—"

"Are you trying to piss me off, Jame?"

"No?" Jamie turns, a look of confusion written all over his handsome face. I give his hand a squeeze, running my thumb over his knuckles.

"You guys aren't mad I didn't tell you the truth about me?"

"What? That you're gay?" Andy leans back in his seat. Jamie nods.

"Why would we be?" Ian asks.

"Because…" It's obvious this is not at all how Jamie expected this to go down.

Experience tells me the longer you hold on to a secret like your sexuality, the greater the fear over coming out becomes. It was one of the factors that led me to coming out at such a young age. I'm sure every single worst-case scenario ran through my boyfriend's mind through the years.

"That you love a man? Who cares?" Pete shrugs. "You *do* love him, right?"

With zero hesitation Jamie says, "With all my heart."

Right back at ya, babe.

"And you feel the same?" Pete directs his question to me.

"Absolutely."

It's Jamie's turn to squeeze my hand.

"That's all that matters, then," Pete states.

Jamie's shoulders have been up by his shoulders, making me want to reach out and massage away the worry. I refrain. For one thing, we aren't much for PDA. And two, if we are going to make it in the long run, he needs to be confident he can handle questions about us on his own. As much as I want to be, I won't always be able to be by side—physically.

I have complete faith in him. He's stronger than he realizes.

"What about the band?" Jamie asks about one of the things I know he was most worried about.

"What about it?" Steve asks.

"Aren't you afraid what me being gay is going to do to the band?"

"Freddie Mercury, David Bowie, Billie Joe Armstrong, Adam Lambert, and Elton John." Ian ticks off a list of names.

"What?"

"All musicians who have successful careers out of the closet."

"*Who* you love has nothing to do with your merit as a musician," Andy says.

"And it sure as shit doesn't change anything for us,"

Pete adds.

"Unless Sammy here decides to be our Yoko Ono, I think we're good," Ian jokes.

Jamie's entire body sags, collapsing against me in relief. I wrap an arm around his back and tuck him tighter to my side. There's a time and place for PDA; this is one of them.

"I *can't* believe you guys don't care." A sense of astonishment laces his words.

"Ehh, it just means less competition with the groupies," Pete says.

"Dude!" Connor shouts, butting in. "I said almost the exact same thing to Sammy when he came out to us. High five." He drops his big body over the couch and holds a hand out to Pete.

I give him a shove, but that doesn't stop the sense of love coming from my family from washing over me.

Soon enough the guys of BoP settle into bro conversation and hockey talk with Connor and Jase.

Using the distraction, Jamie and I slip into one of our private bubbles.

Less than twenty-four hours ago, this wouldn't have been possible. I am so immensely proud of him.

"How do you feel?" I ask.

"Like myself."

I nod in understanding. I felt it when I came out.

"We still have more to deal with." I gesture to all the people dealing with the press fallout.

"I know. But I can handle anything with you by my side."

Damn fucking right.

Chapter 29

Jamie

It only took two days for Jordan and Skye to arrange an interview with *Between the Lyrics*. Though sports are the focus at their firm ATS, they refused to let anyone else—even the record label's PR team—handle the story. When the label tried to step in, they politely told them to go fuck themselves.

When I asked why, Jordan simply responded with, "We take care of our family, no one else." She said it to me, not Sammy.

I was now family.

And I'm more than okay with it.

Now, unlike Jase, I'm not exaggerating when I say every news outlet wanted to be the one to get the exclusive story of my coming out.

It's ridiculous. Who the hell really cares? What difference does it make?

The story shouldn't be who I love but that I'm *in* love. That Jamie Hawke is officially off the market. And damn happy about it.

All the Covenettes are in attendance, but Jordan, Skye and Maddey remain the closest to where the *BTL* people are setting up their camera crew in the media room.

There will be a print article in *Between the Lyrics*, but we are also filming a live piece for their social media platforms, with the hope that the faster the story is out, the quicker people can move on.

Felicity Sparks—the reporter handpicked by Jordan and Skye—sits across from me, Sammy, and the rest of BoP.

With a reassuring smile our way, she nods to the cameraman to start the broadcast.

"For those of you who don't know me, I'm Felicity Sparks, and I have been blessed to have been chosen to be here today. *Between the Lyrics* has been known to bring you the behind-the-scenes stories of triumphs and tragedies for the musical greats through generations."

She talks to the camera as if it's a live audience. She's calm, poised, and relaxed.

"Today I get to tell you all about one of my personal favorites—the love story. For those who have been our faithful subscribers, you know how much I adore a happy ending, and actually, in our midst today we do have an expert on the subject with us"—she shoots a look to where Maddey stands off set— "and if we're *really* lucky we might be able to get her to chime in." She pauses, leaning in closer and cupping her mouth with one hand to almost whisper, "In a professional capacity of course."

She winks and from here you can feel that the viewers are charmed.

"Now." She claps her hands together, eyes lighting up like a kid in a candy store. "I'm going to try and keep my fangirling to a minimum, but today I'm here with all five members of Birds of Prey." She fans herself. "And as if that isn't enough hotness to melt your computer screens, our sixth guest will finish the job."

Andy snorts, Steve snickers, and Pete reaches out to ruffle Sammy's hair, but I smack it away before he can make contact.

"Oh you boys are going to be a handful, aren't you?" She laughs.

"That's what she said." A pained groan can be heard from Jordan at Ian's comment.

"We should have never agreed to do this live." I give Felicity an apologetic look. I can already hear the voice clips and see the GIFs made from the shitshow this has the potential to turn into.

"I grew up with six siblings, I think I can handle them." The smile on her face is genuine. "You good for me to start?"

"Have at it." I lean back in my seat.

"For those of you who haven't seen the news stories the last couple of days, Jamie Hawke, lead singer of Birds of Prey, has been making headlines. Now I know most of you are like, 'But how is that news, Felicity?' and I would have to agree. BoP has been a household name for years, but this time the stories have been focused on a more personal level.

"I'm sure there are countless questions, but since this is my interview, I get to ask what I *really* want to know." She crosses her legs, propping an elbow on the arm of her chair, resting her chin on her fist, like we are old friends settling in for a night of gossip and not a magazine interview. "How did you two meet?"

Not the question I expected.

"We met when Sammy was hired to produce our latest album," I answer.

"And was it love at first sight?"

I look to my boyfriend, those caramel eyes extra melty as he holds back a laugh.

"Not love. But definitely lust."

"What about you, Sammy?" She shifts her focus.

"Well, it was different for me. The day I was brought on as a producer may have been the first time I met Jam, but I'd obviously seen him before."

"Jam?" She picks up on my nickname.

"Oh, shit." Pete groans. "Here come the pet names."

"Pet names?" Her focus shifts again.

"Ignore him." I wave him off. "He's just jealous he doesn't have one."

"So…who asked who out?"

"Umm…" Sammy starts, his brow scrunching.

"You know, I don't think either of us *technically* asked the other."

"True. You kissed me and that was all she wrote, so to say."

"So it was a storybook beginning?" She is visibly swooning.

Sammy snorts. "Yeah, no. This guy"—he hooks his thumb at me—"thought I was dating my best friend when we first met. My *female* best friend."

Maddey attempts to smother her giggles, but when Jordan and Skye lose it, she gives up.

Told you it was going to be a shitshow.

"Can I ask a personal question?" Felicity focuses on Sammy again.

"Isn't that what this whole thing is all about?" He circles a finger, indicating the interview set up.

"Good point." She chuckles.

"But, yes. You can ask me a personal question."

"Were you closeted as well?" There's zero judgment in her voice, and I can see why they picked her as our interviewer.

"No." Sammy glances at me, his eyes softening with affection, and all I want to do is kiss his face. "I've been out since middle school. But a lot of people assume I'm straight because I don't fit the stereotypical mold of what society 'deems gay.'"

"Is that what happened for you when you met?" This time she asks me.

"That and the fact that when we walked into our meeting with him, he was on the phone with Maddey, telling her he loved her." I take Sammy's hand in mine in a rare display of public affection. "But really, I was so attracted to him I wanted to believe there was no possibility of us, because if there was…it would mean admitting the truth about myself."

"That you're gay?"

My hand gets squeezed.

"Yes, and…" I look over my shoulder at my bandmates before continuing. "Mostly I was scared what it would mean for the band or how they would react."

"Which was dumb." Pete throws a hand in the air. I have a feeling he's going to give me shit about not telling him sooner for a while.

"So dumb," Andy agrees.

"But they've been great," I continue like they didn't speak.

"We're family," Ian adds.

"Yeah. Who the hell cares *who* you love? All we care about is that you're happy."

"Are you?" Felicity brings the interview back around.

A smile stretches across my face.

"The happiest."

She mirrors my expression. "Well, I'll tell you this." She leans in as if imparting a juicy secret. "Hearing that will break countless hearts around the globe." Her focus goes back to the camera. "But this reporter couldn't be happier. I love a happy ending. And honestly, one hot prince is good—how do you get any better when there are two of them?" She winks, and the broadcast cuts off.

Sammy and I may not be riding off into the sunset together, but what we have is even better.

Time to live our happily ever after.

Epilogue

Sammy

"Samz." The mattress bounces underneath me as my best friend jumps like she's doing a cannonball onto it. "Oh, Samz."

I roll over with a groan, laying an arm over my eyes to shield them from the sun trying to blind them, and ease one open to glower at my rude as fuck human alarm clock. "Madz."

"Ooo." A finger flicks the barbell pierced through my nipple. "Somebody's a Grumpy Gus this morning," Maddey singsongs.

There are days I wonder why I chose her to be my best friend.

"Why are you in bed with me and *not* my boyfriend?"

I probably only have myself to blame. It was my suggestion to stay at her place down the shore after the band returned from their mini-tour last night.

"Oh, shut up. You know you missed me."

I slick my tongue over my teeth and roll to face the blonde pain in my ass. "Only because there's *clearly* something wrong with me."

Icy blue eyes sparkle with a kind of mischief that would make a weaker man's balls retreat inside their body, but after two decades with this one by my side, I've been conditioned to jump on board with her insanity.

"He's still in bed?"

"Madz, you're slacking."

Both the question and the comment are the only warning I get before the other two main ladies in my life are taking up the last of the available space on the mattress.

"He's too busy complaining I'm not Jamie to get his buns of steel in gear," Maddey says with a huff and a hair flip.

Jordan's hazel eyes assess me with that mama bear intensity she's always been known for and has only intensified since giving birth to her twins a few months ago. "Eh...can't say I blame him on that one, Madz."

"Truth," Skye quickly agrees. "Jamie is *beyond* lickable."

The three of them dissolve into laughter which ends up triggering my own. Still, none of them give me the answer I want.

"Can you guys..." I wave *Go away* hands at them. Guess what? None of them move.

"Look..." I sigh, trying to think of a way out because I know telling them I'm naked beneath the covers will not deter them in the least.

"Aw, is somebody getting shy on us?" Skye hooks a finger inside the edge of the sheet bunched near my waist.

See what I mean?

Thankfully, Jordan takes pity on me and corrals the other two. With three consecutive pats on my ass, they make their way off the bed and out of the room after telling me to "hurry up."

I have no clue what they are up to, but I guess there's only one way to find out.

Epilogue

Jamie

Do you have any idea how it feels to be judged by a head tilt? Well...that's where I'm at. It doesn't help that the canine currently doing the head tilting is more intelligent than some humans I've met.

"You're not helping," I complain.

One ear flips inside out, and the angle of Trident's head tilt ratches up with every step of my continued pacing. If it were possible, I would swear he just rolled his eyes at me.

"He'll say yes, right?" I ask, running a hand down my face.

I may be the crazy person seeking counsel from a dog, but I've never been more nervous about anything in my life. And coming from a guy who only recently had the balls to come out of the closet, that's saying a whole fucking lot.

Trident couldn't care less about my inner turmoil and stretches out a paw for the stuffed sea turtle near his nautical-printed doggie bed.

Squeak. Squeak. Squeak.

Oh, great. Now I have a soundtrack to my pacing.

"Will you chill, Jame?" Pete calls out, watching me from over the rim of his coffee cup like I *am* a crazy person. To be fair, he's probably right.

"What if he says no?" I make another circuit around the couch.

"He's not going to say no." Andy hides a smile behind

his hand.

"But what if he does?" I shoot him a glare, not appreciating him laughing at my expense while I'm a jittery mess.

"He won't," Ian drolls, scrolling through his phone.

"But—"

"He won't," Steve repeats.

My steps come to a stop, and my hands slap the sides of my thighs at how blasé they are all being. "How do you *know*?" I end with a shout.

Four men and one canine sigh, all of them—dog included—share a look that I swear asks, *When did he become so dramatic?*

When did these losers become the least helpful bunch of assholes?

My bandmates bounce a running commentary about my mental state between them and take side bets on when they think I'll completely lose it while I mutter to myself about how much they suck.

Pass after pass, I round Maddey's couch, the area rug in the center of the room bears the evidence of just how restless I am. I'm making yet another rotation around, my footsteps following the path worn into the pile of the rug when a pixie-like female steps in front of me.

"Calm your tits, Jame." A hand comes up to pat my chest. Which are not tits, by the way. Sure, my pecs might be leaner and nowhere close to my boyfriends' broad strength, but I reiterate... they are *not* tits.

My glower game must be weak because all Maddey does is laugh as she settles into her circular reading chair in the corner of the room with the other two ladies.

"Her delivery may need work." Skye shares a smirk with Maddey before redirecting her attention back to me. "But her advice is solid."

"He loves you, Jame. He's not going to say no." The simple, steadfast nature of Jordan's statement hits home in a way nobody else's could. "So why don't you take a breath. He can't say yes if you're too busy hyperventilating to ask in the first place."

Ugh! Fine. They want me to breathe? I'll breathe.

With my hands hanging by my sides, I keep my posture loose and concentrate on pulling oxygen in through my nose, letting it fill each tiny pocket of tissue inside my lungs as if I'm on stage, ready to belt out that final, killer note that will close out the show, before releasing it in a steady stream out of my mouth.

I repeat the process three more times before the sound of footsteps has me whipping around to face the hallway leading to the front of the house.

All the tension gathered between my shoulder blades disappears the second my eyes latch onto a sleep-rumpled Sammy.

I cast a semi-chastising glance at Maddey over my shoulder, but when she shrugs, I can't fully complain that she didn't deliver the directive of getting dressed for the day. How can I when I'm graced with the sight of my fine as fuck boyfriend in a pair of low-slung athletic shorts, the dark gray band of his boxer briefs visible above the waistband, and nothing else? You heard that right—*nothing* else. Every inch of his now bronzed from the sun skin, black ink decorating the sides of his ribs, and topped by twin steel bars through his nipples muscular torso is on display.

I'm nodding my acquiescence before Maddey even finishes whispering, "You're welcome."

Yeah, she's right. I can't be mad at that sight. Especially when that smile that lights up my entire world blooms swift and sure on Sammy's face when he spots me amongst those we're closest to.

"We're going to have to look into getting our own place if we're going to make the shore part of our regular rotation." The roughness lingering in his voice from sleep and the hand absentmindedly scratching at his six-pack distract me from the actual words Sammy is speaking.

"Why's that, Spins?" I ask when they finally register inside my brain.

This time he's the one shooting quasi-dirty looks to his best friend. "Because..." A hand comes up to cup the side of my neck a second before a quick hello kiss hits my lips. "I much prefer being woken up by *you* next to me in bed than that"—he jerks a chin at the ladies—"trouble-making threesome."

"I could get down with some threesome act—*ooff.*" Andy's words cut off with a grunt as Pete elbows him in the gut.

I ignore our bickering friends—again—and keep Sammy close with a lazy hand resting on his hip.

Warm caramel eyes tinged with sleepiness bounce over the features of my face, but that smile never loses its wattage. Any nervousness I felt, all those doubts I had are gone. *Poof!* No more.

How could I ever think he would say no?

It's official. I'm an idiot.

"Not that I don't love you guys or anything..." Sammy says to my bandmates. "But why are you all here?"

I get it. It's been less than twenty-four hours since our mini-tour ended, but I knew I couldn't do this without his girls around too.

Clearing my throat, I rock back onto my heels and reach inside my pocket. I feel around until my finger slips through the cool metal, hooking the tip around the free-floating ring and pulling it out.

Feminine squeals become our soundtrack, but it's the whistling of air as Sammy sucks in a stunned breath that has my full attention.

God, I hope he's not disappointed with how I plan to do this.

We're not the hearts and flowers type. And outside of the *one* interview we granted, neither of us feels the need for any grand gestures when it comes to declaring our love.

Still...

Here's hoping he thinks this fits...us.

"Jam," Sammy breathes, the reverent way he says my name sends a bolt of pleasure shooting down my spine.

Pinching the dark gray Tungsten ring between my fingers,

I take a second to watch the way the light reflects off the vein of black fire opal running through the center.

It's now or never.

"I know I'm a songwriter, and I should be able to craft all manner of epic words." I pause to take a breath. "But anytime I sat down to write, I could only come up with one thing."

I feel like a bumbling fool tripping over my words, but when I finally lift my gaze to Sammy's, his is dancing.

The air moves around us as he shifts closer, his body heat infusing my system as he asks, "What was it?"

My hand flexes at my side, and then I'm reaching for him, my fingers skimming down the back of his arm, feeling every bulge and sinew of muscle on the path to his hand to thread our fingers together.

"I love you."

Freddie Mercury sings from the intensity Sammy's smile takes on. "I love you too."

There was never any doubt about that.

"This may sound selfish, but you make me a better person."

There's a pinch around my knuckles as he squeezes my hand. "You say that like you don't make me better too."

Of course, he would say that; because he's perfect for me.

"Well then..." A nervous chuckle escapes me, and I hold up the ring between us. "How about we keep on making each other better for the rest of our lives? Marry me?"

There are girlish squeals and people shushing, but they only serve as background noise to the only words I want to hear.

"You're goddamn right I will."

Are you one of the cool people who writes reviews? *Musical Mayhem can be found on Amazon, Goodreads, and BookBub.*

Want more BTU Alumni? *All your favorites are back in BTU2- Tap Out.*

Is that too long for your next BTU Alumni fix? Jordan and Lyle have cameos in the #UofJ Series Looking To Score, Game Changer, and Playing For Keeps.

Randomness For My Readers

For anyone who has read <u>Tap Out</u> or stalks me in my reader group, you may know that *Tap Out* was never actually meant to be part of the BTU world when I first started writing it. Once I switched things up, it just felt right for Sammy to be married.

So last year, when I got the chance to be a part of the Rule Breaker Antho, I knew I had to go back and write his and Jamie's story.

In my acknowledgments, I give a shout-out to one of my favorite authors to read, and fangirl talk to, Cambria Hebert. I fell in love with MM romance by chance through her books, and now I'm an addict. I love the emotions inside MM romance. And, not going to lie, I was HUGELY intimidated to try and write this book.

If this was your first book of mine, there's a lot more in store for this squad. So meet them all in *Power Play*. And then get to see Sammy and Jamie peeks of them as husbands throughout the rest of the series, all free to read in KU.

If my rambling hasn't turned you off and you are like, "This chick is my kind of crazy," feel free to reach out!

Lots of Love,
Alley

Acknowledgments

Don't tell the Hubs but this is the first acknowledgments that he's not the first, but that honor goes to all you, the readers, who loved Sammy and Jamie so much that you wanted to know their story even though they were an established couple. I freaking heart you.

Now the man who holds down the fort and keep the tiny humans known as the mini royals alive while I get lost in with my characters. Love you babe.

To my Beta Bitches, my OG Coven, our Coven Conversations give me life.

To Bree, Lillian, and Sierra for being my extra eyes and making sure my first MM came up to snuff.

To Jenny my PA, without her I wouldn't be organized enough for any of my releases to happen. Thank you for being the other half of my brain and video chatting all hours, damn our timezones and letting me break your heart over and over with this book. You know I live for your shouty capitals.

To Sarah for being my graphics queen *always.*

To Sandra from One Love Editing for taking on my crazy and editing this bad boy for me.

To Gemma for going from my proofreader to fangirl and being so invested in my characters stories to threaten my life *lovingly of course* I can't even begin to tell you how entertained I was by all your hockey questions.

To Cambria Hebert for being the first author whose MM book I read years ago with my favorite couple #TrewLove, making me fall in love with the trope so much I had to write my own.

To my street team for being the best pimps ever. Seriously, you guys rock my socks.

To my ARC team for giving my books some early love and getting the word out there.

To every blogger and bookstagrammer that takes a chance and reads my words and writes about them.

Thank you to all the authors in the indie community for your continued support. I am so happy to be a part of this amazing group of people.

To my fellow Covenettes for making my reader group one of my happy places. Whenever you guys post things that you know belong there I squeal a little.

And, of course, to you my fabulous reader, for picking up my book and giving me a chance. Without you I wouldn't be able to live my dream of bringing to life the stories the voices in my head tell me.

Lots of Love,
Alley

For A Good Time Call

Did you have fun meeting The Coven? Do you want to stay up-to-date on releases, be the first to see cover reveals, excerpts from upcoming books, deleted scenes, sales, freebies, and all sorts of insider information you can't get anywhere else?

Ask yourself this:

* Are you a Romance Junkie?

* Do you like book boyfriends and book besties? (yes this is a thing)

* Is your GIF game strong?

* Want to get inside the crazy world of Alley Ciz?

If any of your answers are yes, maybe you should join my Facebook reader group, Romance Junkie's Coven

About The Author

Alley Ciz is an internationally bestselling indie author of sassy heroines and the alpha men that fall on their knees for them. She is a romance junkie whose love for books turned into her telling the stories of the crazies who live in her head...even if they don't know how to stay in their lane.

This Potterhead can typically be found in the wild wearing a funny T-shirt, connected to an IV drip of coffee, stuffing her face with pizza and tacos, chasing behind her 3 minis, all while her 95lb yellow lab—the best behaved child—watches on in amusement.